"Personally, I've had it with romance.

"Love doesn't last," Caroline said. "It's all just an illusion."

Jack had no trouble understanding her now—that was his own philosophy. "What about attraction?" he asked, his masculine interest sparked. "How do you handle that?"

Caroline gave him a quick look. "Let's just say that I don't trust attraction."

"Do you mean you just don't trust men?" he asked.

"Let's say I stopped believing in fairy tales."

"Cinderella home from the ball, huh?" His tone was soft.

"I've never quite thought of myself as a Cinderella."

"Maybe that's because the right Prince Charming hasn't come along."

Dear Reader,

Silhouette Romance has a new look and we'd love to know if you like it! We've updated our covers, but inside you'll find the same heartwarming, satisfying love stories we know our readers look forward to each and every month. Silhouette Romance novels emphasize the traditional values of family, commitment . . . and the special kind of love that is destined to last forever. We hope our new covers say that to you.

Inside our bright new wrapping, you'll find delightful romances by Joleen Daniels, Val Whisenand and Pat Tracy. And in the spirit of our cover launch, we're introducing two talented newcomers to the line, Jude Randal and Jayne Addison.

In this month's WRITTEN IN THE STARS, we're featuring the steadfast Virgo man in Karen Leabo's *A Changed Man.* And in the months to come, watch for stories by your favorite authors, including Diana Palmer, Annette Broadrick, Marie Ferrarella and many, many more.

The Silhouette Romance authors and editors love to hear from readers and we'd love to hear from *you.*

Happy reading from all of us at Silhouette!

Valerie Susan Hayward
Senior Editor

YOU MADE ME LOVE YOU

Jayne Addison

Published by Silhouette Books New York
America's Publisher of Contemporary Romance

For Steven, Andrew and Beth, as always.

SILHOUETTE BOOKS
300 E. 42nd St., New York, N.Y. 10017

YOU MADE ME LOVE YOU

ISBN: 0-373-08888-4

First Silhouette Books printing September 1992

Printed in the U.S.A.

JAYNE ADDISON

lives on the North Shore of Long Island with her husband, Jerome. Their three children, Steven, Andrew and Beth, are presently attending colleges away from home. Between running up huge phone bills talking to the kids, Jayne fills her free time away from a full-time job as a salesperson/bookkeeper for a local builder by writing romance fiction. It's one way to beat the empty-nest syndrome.

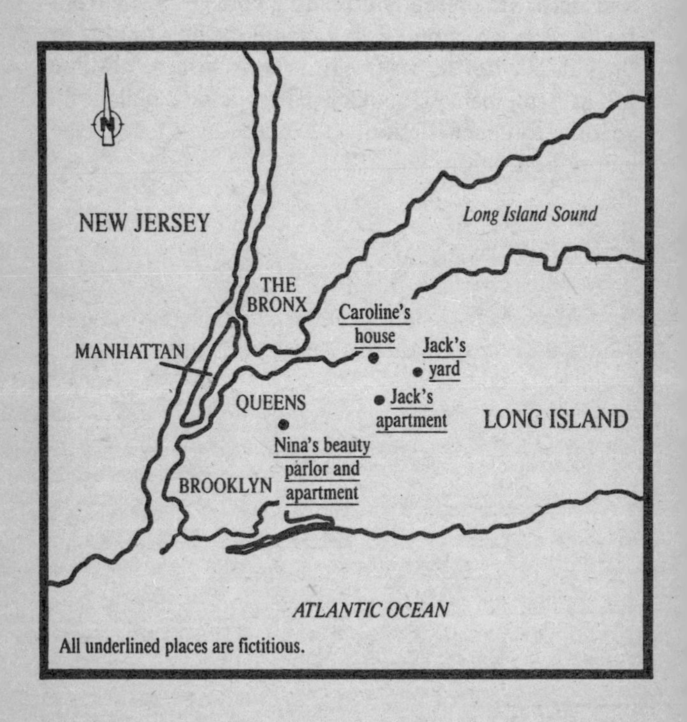
NEW JERSEY
Long Island Sound
THE
BRONX
Caroline's
house
Jack's
yard
MANHATTAN
QUEENS
Jack's
apartment
LONG ISLAND
Nina's beauty
parlor and
apartment
BROOKLYN
ATLANTIC OCEAN
All underlined places are fictitious.

Chapter One

Jack Corey set his suitcase on the floor. He'd been out of town for over a week, and his studio apartment was stuffy. He opened a couple of windows, but there was hardly a breeze outside.

He was glad to be back on Long Island. The grading job that he'd just bulldozed with fill for a friend in New Jersey had been more of a push than he'd expected. Of course, with the way his luck had been going lately, he should have figured there'd be problems.

He pulled his wallet out of the pocket of his jeans, dropping it on his desk after removing the check that was folded inside. Jack mentally subtracted the added expenses he'd incurred while looking at the amount on the check. It was a wonder that he'd come out making anything at all on the job.

He glanced at his answering machine. It registered two messages. He settled himself in his swivel chair and swung his legs onto the top of the desk. Rotating his shoulders against the crick of pain making its way down his back, Jack rewound the tape and set it to play.

"Hi, this is Caroline Phelps. It's nine-thirty, Saturday morning, September 10. Just a minute... *Elizabeth, you can't wash the dog with Ajax.* Now, where was I? Oh, yes. The reason I'm calling... *Get him out of the living room. Bobby, stop shaking the cleansing powder on him. No, don't pour water on him in there. Take him outside. Bobby, watch out for the can of paint. The lid's not on tight. Oh, no...*" The message ended as she disconnected.

Jack switched off the machine for a minute and grinned, picturing the scene that Caroline Phelps had just described—the kids, the dog and a can of paint. Then his brow creased. He wondered why she'd called.

Knowing full well that he could easily think up trouble, Jack glanced around his studio apartment to avoid thinking at all. The place was pretty much a mess. The convertible couch was still opened into a bed. The two pillows he'd punched out the last time he'd slept here were tossed to the floor. Jack debated whether or not to straighten up, then decided it could wait. It wasn't as if he were expecting any company.

The doorbell rang just as he went to turn the answering machine back on.

"I'll be right there," Jack called out as he got to his feet. He grabbed his pillows up from the floor and flung them into a closet.

The doorbell rang again, followed by the slightly accented voice of Nina Sanchez. "I got my hands full," she said impatiently. "Hurry up."

Jack opened the door and smiled. The sixty-one-year-old dynamo who was five-foot-two in her two-inch heels had been a mother to him ever since he was fifteen. He adored her, and he knew she cared as much about him as she did her natural son, Ray. Ray, who was six months Jack's junior, was as close to him as a brother.

Nina handed him the brown paper bag she was holding sideways and whisked in. "Put it in the refrigerator," she instructed in her take-charge manner.

"What's in here?" Jack asked, walking around the oak counter and stools that separated the living room-bedroom from the kitchenette.

"I made you some *arroz con pollo,*" Nina answered, glancing around. The room was decorated in beige and white, chrome and bleached wood.

"Thanks, Momma," Jack said, coming back into the main room after putting the food away. "You know how much I love your cooking."

She was delighted with his flattery. "I know." She nodded nonchalantly. Then she walked over to his convertible couch and started to yank the sheets off the bed. She was not the kind of woman who could just stand around doing nothing.

Smiling, Jack stepped in her way. "I think I'm a bit too old for you to pick up after me."

"Don't think I'm planning to make a habit of this," came her retort as she dropped his sheets to the carpeted floor.

Jack grabbed the end of the bed frame, folding the sections into a couch before Nina could get her hands on it. Never idle, Nina took one of the cushions propped against the back of the couch and set it into place. Jack set up the other one. Nina sat down and looked up to study him over the rim of the tortoise-shell glasses perched on the tip of her nose.

"What?" Jack asked, after good-naturedly accepting a moment's inspection.

Nina continued to eye him thoughtfully. "I'm worried about you."

"There's no reason for you to be worried about me. I'm fine." He stood looking relaxed, his hands idly crossed in front of his broad chest.

"Are you saying that you're over her?"

"It's been six months."

"That's not an answer."

"Okay. Other than still feeling like a sap, I'm fine." Jack's stance didn't change, but he could feel his muscles tighten. Not that he wasn't over her. But how did he get over the humiliation of being jilted practically at the altar?

Nina stood up and gave his cheek a gentle touch. "It's not easy to know when love is real. With all the women that have chased around after you, you just picked the wrong one. She wasn't right for you, anyway."

Jack's mouth lifted with a rueful smile. He'd figured that out for himself. Only he couldn't take much credit for it—he'd only figured it out with hindsight.

Nina gave Jack a compassionate look as she continued, "You've got to check the feet. That's your first clue about a woman."

"Really? What am I looking for?" Jack asked, picking up his sheets from the floor.

"Small feet—big heart," Nina explained matter-of-factly.

Jack grinned as he took his sheet to the bathroom hamper. "After all this time, you tell me *now* that I should be checking out a woman's feet?"

"Didn't I have to help Ray see that Gloria was right for him?" Nina asked rhetorically as Jack came back. "You watch, pretty soon now, he's going to ask her to marry him."

"Momma, you can play matchmaker with Ray if he'll let you, but don't you go playing matchmaker with me. Anyway, I've decided that I'm through with romance for a while... a long while. I think I'll just enjoy my bachelor status. Besides, I've got to devote all my time and energy to this new business deal Ray and I have on the fire."

Nina waved a finger at him. "That's no way to talk. You can't push romance aside. You're thirty-two years old, and you should be married, starting a family, not just running around. What you have to do is find the right woman... one who doesn't have dollar signs on her mind."

Jack grinned. "Momma, when it comes down to the bottom line, they all have dollar signs on their minds. I think I'll just stick to running around, if I even find time for it." He wasn't being cynical. He was just smarter than he'd been a year ago.

Nina sighed her aggravation. "I don't know what to do with you." She ruffled his hair. "I hope you know you need a haircut. And when was the last time you shaved?"

Jack ran rough fingers through his unruly blondish-brown hair. He was way overdue for a trim, and he hadn't shaved in two days.

Nina watched him. "Get me a pair of scissors."

"I'll come by the shop during the week. You can cut my hair then." Nina owned a small beauty parlor in Queens.

"I'm here now. It will only take me a few minutes."

Jack didn't see any point in arguing. "Okay, but just let me go shave first." His long-legged athletic stride took him back to the bathroom.

Nina watched Jack lather his face through the open door. "Ray told me some of the equipment broke down and it cost you a lot of money to get it fixed. And now

Ray is mad at you because you paid him his salary and didn't let him share the loss."

"Ray won't stay mad at me for long. You know that."

"Of course he won't stay mad at you. Do brothers stay mad?"

Jack took out a razor from the medicine cabinet. "I should have expected something to go wrong on the job. It's becoming the story of my life."

"Oh, pooh..."

"Pooh?" Jack grinned, then groaned as he nicked his jaw.

"You did get the house sold, finally."

"I first close on it tomorrow. And if anything, that proves my point. I buy a house in a seller's market and pay top-dollar, and then when I go to sell it—not only is it a buyer's market, but a gas station comes in down the street, making it almost impossible to get rid of. And there I am, having sunk every extra dollar I had into it to keep the mortgage low so Jill and I could have lived easy. How's that for luck?" For a split second Jack let himself think about Jillian Gates. Jack and Jill... What a joke!

He thought back to the week before he was supposed to get married, when Jill had decided she wanted out. An old boyfriend of hers had come back on the scene—an old, *rich* boyfriend—and Jill had realized she was still in love with him.

"Well, once I close on the house tomorrow with Caroline Phelps, maybe my luck will change." Jack cocked his head to the left and worked the razor over the opposite side of his jaw.

"Is she living alone in the house?"

"No, she's got two kids, and there's an older woman who lives with them and takes care of the kids while she's at work."

"Is she a widow or divorced?" Nina's husband had died nearly fourteen years ago.

"She's divorced."

"And she had the money to buy a house?"

"The real estate agent told me that she'd gotten the down payment from her divorce settlement. It must have been a fairly large settlement." Jack popped his head out the door. "Women—they get you either coming or going. I guess it pays not to make too much money."

Nina made a face at him. "Stop talking that way. Besides, you've done all right for yourself with your business."

Jack went back to shaving. "I'm looking to do better than just 'all right.' And I will when the deal Ray and I have in the works takes off."

Nina tried a different approach to the same subject. "How come you let her move into the house before you closed?"

"She wanted to get the kids into school for the beginning of September, and since the bank needed more time to get all the paperwork done, I agreed to let her rent the house. We were only talking about a month." Jack stuck his head back out the door and winked. "Didn't you already give me this third-degree?"

"All you told me was that she's an actress. By the way, I saw her on TV. She's very pretty. She doesn't have a very big part on the soap, but she's a new character. You never know."

Jack splashed cold water on his face, dried himself off and dabbed three cuts with toilet paper. "I don't want to know. All I want is to close on the house with her and put that money into that subdivision deal with Dick Taylor. I'm just going to make it with that and the rest of the money I have on the side." Once he and Ray were part of that building combine, they'd be sitting pretty.

Nina took off the two bracelets she was wearing and placed them on a glass end table. "Take your shirt off and put a towel around your shoulders. Where are your scissors?"

"There should be a pair in the top drawer of my desk." Jack pulled his white T-shirt up over his head, grabbed a comb and walked out of the bathroom wearing a towel around his neck.

"So, what's she like in real life?" Nina questioned, finding the scissors under an array of scattered papers in Jack's desk drawer. "Is she as pretty as she is on TV?"

"All I noticed was that she had huge feet," Jack teased with mock innocence as he sat down on the couch.

Nina smacked Jack lightly across the back of his head. "Don't be a smart aleck!"

Jack grinned. "All right, she's pretty."

"No," Nina said decisively.

"No, she's not pretty?"

"I'm just saying that she's not for you. Actresses."

"What about actresses?"

"I read *People*. I see the talk shows. They're wild, reckless, irresponsible..."

"She didn't strike me as being wild or irresponsible. If anything, she impressed me as being levelheaded, down to earth, cool, calm and collected. She seems very devoted to her children."

Nina's eyes lit up. "Oh, well...so maybe they're not all bad."

Feeling frazzled and disoriented, Caroline stepped gingerly around some still-unopened cartons in her bedroom. Preoccupied with her thoughts, she missed the corner of one and stubbed her toe. She muttered under her breath and blamed Jack Corey for her mishap. He was so much on her mind, she wasn't able to concentrate on anything else.

Every time the phone rang, she was sure it was him. She concluded he was out of town, knowing that he'd be calling her as soon as he heard her message on his machine. She was dreading his call, wishing they'd hit it off a little better the other few times they'd talked.

Hobbling by an unhung mirror propped up against one of the walls, Caroline stupidly stopped to scrutinize herself. In the mood she was in she didn't see a nice, delicate face with a clear, creamy complexion, a trim, shapely body, and wavy cinnamon hair devoid of split ends. All she could see was a thirty-year-old blah. She focused on her hair. She was still wearing it in the same style she'd had since her teens—cut to her shoulders, tucked behind her ears, with wispy bangs that more often than not got in the way of her vision. Her old and faded cranberry cotton robe with its pulled hem hanging unevenly around her knees wasn't helping her image any. However, her attire was perfect for the messy job she had ahead of her.

Standing at the open door, Jack bent down and gave Nina an affectionate hug and a kiss on her cheek. He had his T-shirt back on, and his hair was trimmed just the way he liked it—still a little long, but less unruly.

"I wouldn't be leaving you so soon, but I'm opening up the beauty parlor this afternoon." Nina tapped her dark hair, checking for any loose ends. She wore it high on her head in a topknot.

Jack caught a strand and tucked it into place. "Since when do you work on Sundays?"

"I'm doing a favor for Dolores Martinez. She has an important date for tonight with a new boyfriend. Did you ever meet Dolores?" Nina had that matchmaker look in her eyes.

"You never give up," Jack countered with a grin.

"I know." Nina smiled. "So what are you going to do today?"

"Listen to the rest of the messages on my answering machine and think about how my luck is going to change after I close on the house tomorrow."

"Find a good woman and your luck will change." Turning on her heels, Nina left him with that last bit of sage advice.

A slight trace of impatience showed on Jack's face as he closed the door. Love—that was a laugh. He didn't believe in love, not anymore. Going back to his desk, he sat down and turned his answering machine back on.

"Hi, this is Caroline Phelps...again. It's Saturday, the tenth. The reason I'm calling... Well... You see... There's this problem—not a big problem. Anyway, I'm not going to be able to close on the house on the nineteenth as we scheduled..." She hesitated, then added quickly. "I guess you'd better call me when you get back. My number is 555-6215."

Groaning out loud, Jack turned his answering machine off and reached for his phone. What did she mean, she wasn't going to be able to close on the house tomorrow? The deal with Dick Taylor depended on him getting that money.

Caroline walked barefoot down the polished oak stairs to the first floor of the house. She padded through the living room, intentionally glancing down. It had taken a half a can of turpentine to get the mauve paint off the wood floor. As if she didn't have enough to do, what with all the rest of the cartons still to unpack—now she was going to have to refinish the floor. Still, she smiled as she gazed around. She loved this old Victorian house with its front porch and oddly shaped extensions. There were all sorts of places for the kids to hide and play—Elizabeth with her dolls and Bobby with his model planes and rocket ships.

Caroline wondered what the two of them were up to at the moment. It was too quiet in the house.

She found them in the large, old-fashioned kitchen. Elizabeth was on the phone. Bobby was standing next to her making faces as he tried to listen in at the receiver.

"Who are you talking to?" Caroline gave her two impish kids a cautious look.

Bobby raised brown eyes up from beneath a mop of sandy hair. "If Elizabeth can make calls then I can, too."

Her nine-year-old son and seven-year-old daughter always vied to keep things even between them.

Caroline signaled in on her daughter. "I hope you aren't calling that nursery rhyme phone number after I told you not to." Those calls cost a fortune.

Elizabeth nodded her head, sending her long, chocolate-brown curls bouncing.

"Hang up the phone," Caroline said firmly.

"But I didn't hear the end," Elizabeth complained as she replaced the receiver.

Caroline smiled wryly. "They all lived happily ever after." They always did... in fairy tales. *She* couldn't even keep a romance alive on a TV soap, let alone in real life.

"But I wanted to hear it," Elizabeth whined.

With a sigh, Caroline poured herself a cup of black coffee. "Why aren't the two of you playing with Maxie? You both wanted a dog. Where is Maxie?"

"He's outside in the back," Bobby answered. "Can I make one call to the Monster line? Elizabeth had her turn."

"No." Caroline used her no-nonsense voice. "I've told you both that those calls are a rip-off. Now, do you each want to pay for them out of your allowance when the bill comes in?"

Bobby grumbled a "no," speaking for himself and his sister, who was shaking her head.

Caroline took a sip of her coffee and then put the cup down to take out a box of tin foil from beneath the sink. "If you don't want to play with Maxie, then how about the two of you planting those marigolds I bought yesterday?"

"Do we have to?" Bobby shuffled his feet, marking up the linoleum with the spiked soles of his AstroTurf sneakers.

"Do we have to?" Elizabeth chimed, mimicking her brother, even though the idea of planting flowers appealed to her.

"Just think how happy Myra is going to be when she comes back from visiting her cousin and she sees those flowers all planted."

"If we plant those dumb flowers can we go to the beach this afternoon and hunt for shells and buried treasure?" Bobby bargained.

"All right." Caroline smiled, allowing herself to be manipulated. "After lunch."

"Can we both invite friends?" Elizabeth asked.

The moment Caroline nodded, her two kids raced for the phone.

After drumming his fingers for five minutes, Jack dialed Caroline Phelps again. The line was still busy. Getting to his feet, Jack frisked himself for the keys to his car. It was only a half-hour drive to the house. He pulled on a light blue denim work shirt, left it unbuttoned and took off.

The directions on the blond-streaking kit were simple enough. Caroline donned the elasticized plastic cap that came in the box. She could hear Elizabeth and Bobby out back now from the opened window in her bathroom. They were doing what came naturally to them—fighting.

Jack Corey came into her thoughts again, not that he'd been far out of them. What would he do when he found out she'd lost her job and that until she got another one, she wouldn't qualify for a mortgage?

She tried to be optimistic. Marty Gold, her agent, had set up two auditions for tomorrow. She might very well have another part by the end of the day. But would the bank clear another mortgage for her right away? The loans officer had said there was a possibility, namely because she was looking to put so much down on the house.

Caroline scanned the instructions on the box one more time. Marty hadn't said she had to be a blonde for the audition, but it might help. If nothing else, maybe it would help her spirits. Didn't blondes have more fun?

Jack revved the motor of his red, three-year-old, two-seater Toyota MR2. Maybe he could delay the deal with Dick Taylor a few more days. But that was it. Whatever Caroline Phelps's problem was, she'd better have a plan to solve it, fast! Muttering to himself, Jack drove off.

Moaning and grimacing, Caroline pulled the last strand of hair through the hole in the plastic cap with the crochet hook that had been supplied. She paused to take a deep breath before applying the bleaching solution and wrapping each strand tightly in tin foil. Whoever had said it hurt to be beautiful had been right. Not that she was expecting to turn out beautiful. Caroline would be more than happy to settle for a new look that had some pizzazz. There was a lot of competition in daytime TV.

Obeying the blue-and-white car behind him, Jack pulled to the side of the road.

"I came to a full stop," Jack insisted when the officer sidled up to his window.

"You rolled," the officer responded dryly. "Let me see your license and registration."

Sucking in an exasperated breath, Jack dug his hands into his pockets, but came up empty. *Terrific,* he was thinking as he said, "I must have left my wallet at home." He remembered exactly where—on his desk.

"Now, isn't that a shame." The officer smiled, only he wasn't amused.

Caroline put a cassette of Frank Sinatra love songs into her portable tape recorder. She set her alarm clock for ten minutes and then lay facedown on her bed so as not to disturb her tin-foiled head. She closed her eyes, just to rest. Worrying had kept her awake most of the night. She tried to fantasize about how she was going to look with her hair streaked, but she couldn't come up with a vision. Instead, she came up with a clear picture of Jack Corey, with his sun-bleached dirty-blond hair and incredible blue eyes. She'd been surprised to learn he was single. Why, she wondered, hadn't some hot number snapped him up? Maybe he didn't want to be snapped up. Not that she was interested one way or the other. She had far more pressing problems on her mind—like having a steady job, providing a stable, healthy environment for her children, seeing to it that she made it as Super Mom.

Jack's brakes squealed as he parked his car at the curb. He got out, slamming the door behind him. He was not in the best of moods as he headed for the front of the house. From the backyard, he could hear Caroline's two kids with their voices raised. Thinking she might be out back with them, Jack changed direction and walked over to the opened gate of the fence. He saw her son holding the hose. The little girl was arguing that she wanted to water the flowers. They were both wearing bathing suits.

"Is your mother in the house?" Jack called out.

"Yes," Bobby answered, almost losing his grip on the hose as he turned his head to glance at Jack.

Jack left them playing or fighting—he couldn't tell which—and went up the porch steps to the front door. He rang the bell. Right at that moment, Elizabeth came running out of the gate. She was screaming as Bobby chased her with the hose, trying to get her wet.

"Okay, kids. Calm down," Jack said, stepping away from the front door to intercede.

Elizabeth darted toward Jack.

Bobby aimed.

Elizabeth sidestepped.

Jack got the blast from the hose.

Caroline woke with a start to a ringing sound. Her head still on the pillow, she reached out for her alarm clock and hit the button. The ringing continued over the music of the cassette tape. Disoriented, she pushed herself up to a sitting position and then distinguished the sound. It was the doorbell.

Shaky-legged, Caroline waved her way down the stairs to the front door. The bell was still ringing. Whoever it was didn't know the meaning of patience. Annoyed, she yanked open the door.

Jack took his finger off the bell. His jaw was clenched. Water from his hair was dripping into his eyes.

It took Caroline a fraction of a second before she recognized him. "What happened to you?" she asked. It wasn't raining outside.

"Your son got me with the hose," Jack answered tersely, slicking his wet hair back with his fingers. It was then that he took a good look at her. "What happened to you?" She looked like she'd stuck her finger into an electrical socket and gotten the full brunt of a shock.

"Me?" Caroline repeated puzzled. Then her hands went to her head and her face colored. She probably looked like a porcupine. "What time is it?" she asked, jangled.

Jack looked at his watch. Fortunately, it was waterproof. "It's nearly noon."

"Oh, my God..." Caroline fled from the door and ran up the stairs screaming. "I can't believe this is happening!" She'd been asleep for nearly an hour.

Reacting automatically, Jack ran after her, expecting to confront some emergency. His wet sneakers squeaked.

Caroline stopped short in her bedroom and picked up her alarm clock. "I can't believe it," she groaned again and looked at Jack. "I had it set to ring on p.m., not a.m." She threw the clock on her bed and charged into the bathroom. Without a thought to closing the door, she started ripping away at the tin foil in her hair.

Jack stood in the bedroom where Sinatra was singing "Only Fools Rush In" at top volume, and debated whether to go downstairs to the living room and wait for her or ask her if she needed any help. He could see she wasn't making much progress getting the tin foil out of her hair, and from the look on her face, she was hurting herself trying to get it all out.

"I think I'd better help you," he said, going in to join her in the bathroom. He fought with her to take her hands down. "What were you trying to do?"

Caroline covered her face with her hands, but she could still see herself sideways in the mirror with her fingers spread. "I was just trying to streak my hair a shade lighter." Her voice quivered. "It was supposed to stay this way for ten minutes, but then I fell asleep and the alarm didn't go off."

The hair Jack was uncovering was straw-white. He suspected that this wasn't the result she'd hoped for, so he waltzed her away from the mirror before she could see for herself.

"It's awful, isn't it?" Caroline asked in total turmoil.

"No," he lied, feeling sorry for her. Water still dripping from his hair got into his eyes, and he blinked.

Caroline gave him a squinting look. "You're lying. I can tell."

Jack smiled. "You don't know me well enough to know how I look when I lie." He had all the tin foil out of her hair, now and he was studying the plastic cup. "Should I take this off?" He fingered the edges.

Miserably, Caroline nodded.

Jack threw the plastic cap to the white ceramic floor, where he'd also thrown the tin foil.

Caroline looked directly into Jack's turquoise eyes. Her bottom lip started to tremble as she fought back tears.

Jack put his arm awkwardly around her shoulder while Sinatra finished the last refrain to "That Old Black Magic Called Love," ending the tape.

"It's going to be all right," he said, offering his best shot at comfort.

"I don't know why I never can get my life together. Something always goes wrong," Caroline mumbled.

Jack smiled wryly. *Tell me about it,* he thought, his heart going out to her. Then, without thinking, he cupped her chin with his hands and gave her a light, reassuring kiss on the cheek.

"It's going to be okay," he said again, his voice a notch huskier.

"I doubt it," Caroline responded forlornly. The lingering touch of his lips to her cheek had been a surprisingly pleasant, but only momentary, distraction. She was too miserable to even attempt to play on his sympathy. Besides, that had never been her style.

She looked wanly up at him. Even with her hair chaotic, he found himself noticing her uniquely appealing face. A bit annoyed with himself for having been observant, Jack backed away, jamming his hip into the bathroom sink.

Caroline's hand went to her hair. Straw. She was afraid to look in the mirror. Tears slipped down her cheeks.

Instantly, Jack moved back closer to her. "You don't look so bad," he said, giving her a quick, easy smile.

"So, I do look bad, just not *so bad?*"

Jack thought of taking her into his arms. "That's not what I meant," he said, deciding to stick with a verbal approach.

Caroline started for the mirror. She'd have to face herself sometime. Jack's hand shot out, stopping her. "Nothing's ever so bad it can't be fixed." His thumb smoothed away some of her tears.

For a moment, Jack's tender touch actually made Caroline forget about her hair and all her other worries. For a moment . . .

"Oh . . . no," she gasped as she finally faced her reflection. "I've ruined my hair. Nothing is going right . . ." she moaned. "What am I going to do . . . ? I've lost my job. I'll never get another part. Myra isn't sure she likes it out here. Elizabeth won't pay attention to her teacher. Now I can't get a mortgage. And the dog won't eat anything but steak. But I can't take him back to the pound because we love him already. And . . ."

"Hold it." Jack put his hands on her shoulders and turned her around. "Could you go over that list once more. Only this time a lot slower.'

Chapter Two

Caroline was squirming as she faced Jack. She was instantly aware that she'd spilled the beans. "I was...fired," she reaffirmed, dejectedly. "The bank won't give me the mortgage. But," she hurried on, trying for an upbeat tone, "but it's only temporary. Just until I land another part." And then she remembered her hair. How could she go on those auditions tomorrow looking the way she did?

"That's just great!" Jack groaned. "How could I be so stupid? I should have known better than to take a woman at her word."

"It wasn't that I broke my word," Caroline said sharply, insulted.

Berating himself, Jack ignored her remark. "Why couldn't I just have waited for that other prospect to get back to me?"

Other prospect? "Oh..." Caroline had a sinking feeling in the pit of her stomach. This wasn't going very well.

"I thought you said the house had been on the market for a while."

"It had been, and I hadn't got any offers. Then in the space of one day, I got two bites."

"Well, maybe the other people would have had trouble getting a mortgage."

"It was a single guy, and he offered me an all-cash deal. All he wanted was a few days to get his finances worked out. But do I give him some time?" Jack shook his head. "You walk in and I take a binder from you instead. And do you want to know why?" He paused for emphasis.

She had a feeling that she didn't, but she nodded her head, anyway.

"I'll tell you why. Because I liked the way you were with your kids, and I liked their excitement over the house. I think you were pretty excited yourself, even though you were trying to act cool." He started to pace out of the bathroom and then back. "I even let you chew me down five thousand bucks...."

"Let me? You didn't let me." She stepped across his stride, catching him back in the bathroom. "I negotiated with you fair and square." *Sexist,* she decided, slapping a label on him. And he was too good-looking for his own good.

"Why'd they fire you, anyway?" Jack demanded. "You told me you were guaranteed five years on that show."

"It was a verbal guarantee. They changed their minds before the contract was drawn up. Anyway, what difference does it make why? These things happen." She didn't add that they seemed to happen to her more frequently than to most.

"Women! They tell you one thing—you believe them—and then *pow*. Just when they've got you where they want you, they pull the rug right out..."

"Listen, if we're going to talk about having rugs pulled out, I've landed flat on my... Well, I've had the rug pulled out on me plenty. By men," she added for emphasis. She was so angry she thumped his chest. "Trust a man to think only about himself, dishing out sympathy only when it's to his advantage, then getting frustrated over situations that no one can control. Worse, they leave you stranded when something better and younger comes along."

She was fighting mad now, and her anger only escalated when she saw his mouth start to curve in a smile. "What's so funny?" she demanded.

Jack couldn't hold back a sudden grin. "You look like a blond spitfire."

Her hand shot again to her hair. She swirled back round to the mirror, her image knocking all the fight right out of her. "Spitfire? I look like—" her voice cracked "—like... Frankenstein after a bad night."

"I do think you'd better wash out that... goopy stuff. Maybe, after a shampoo..."

Caroline turned on the water and dropped her head into the sink. She mumbled something about shampoo.

Jack spotted it on the edge of the bathtub and reached for it. He unscrewed the cap and handed it to her. It slipped from her fingers and fell to the floor, some of the emerald liquid spilling out. Jack picked the bottle up and, feeling like it was the thing to do, poured some over her head. Trying to help her out, he started rubbing it in. He'd never shampooed someone else's hair before, but he'd spent enough hours over the years in Nina's beauty shop and watched her shampoo hundreds of heads.

Caroline grabbed for a towel, as some of the shampoo got into her eyes.

"I can do it myself...." She went to shove him away, but her feet started to go out from under her as she slid on the shampoo that had spilt on the floor. Reflexively, Caroline went to grab on to Jack. He had just started to take a step away and was caught off balance. He went down first, landing in a sitting position on his rear end, Caroline landing across his knees with her legs folded up against the vanity under the sink.

"I think I must be jinxed," Caroline moaned.

"*You're* jinxed...I've probably got a hex on me," Jack countered.

From downstairs, Bobby yelled, "Elizabeth and I are going to make peanut butter and jelly sandwiches, and Myra is home."

Caroline and Jack both tried to get up at the same time, only to find themselves getting more entangled with each other. There wasn't much space to maneuver in the small bathroom.

"Where are you, Caroline?" Myra Cummings yelled anxiously from the doorway of Caroline's bedroom. "Bobby said there's a strange man in the house."

Before Caroline could answer, Myra spotted her young friend and the stranger battling in the bathroom.

Letting out a cry of alarm and moving with surprising quickness for a woman who was in her mid-fifties and more than just pleasingly plump, Myra rushed to Caroline's aid. She raised her purse high in the air and swung her handbag at Jack.

"Wait, Myra. Stop. It's Jack Corey," Caroline said frantically, making a grab for Myra's purse. In her effort to defend Jack, Caroline accidentally punched him in the eye.

Jack cried out in pain and then mumbled something indistinguishable under his breath. Caroline didn't need to understand the words to tell that it wasn't anything endearing.

"What is happening here?" Myra asked, looking confused.

"Myra, it's Jack Corey," Caroline repeated, enunciating her words. "Jack Corey, the man who owns the house—our house."

"Oh, my goodness," Myra said excitedly.

Caroline looked at Jack holding his hand over his right eye. "Did I hurt you?" she asked solicitously. "Are you all right? Let me see."

Jack jumped back a safe ten inches away from her. She was a menace. "It's okay," he said. "This just isn't my day." And then as much to himself as to Caroline, he added, "This just hasn't been my year."

Myra, still befuddled by what was going on, came up to fuss over Jack. "Oh, Mr. Corey, what can we do for you?"

"I think I'll just go down to the kitchen and find some ice. You do have some ice in the refrigerator, I hope?"

"Of course, come along," Myra said sweetly. "I even know where there's an ice pack." She stopped for a moment, observing that Caroline's hair was covered in a sea of lather. She shook her head in bewilderment. "I don't know why you'd be washing your hair with company in the house."

Jack was holding an ice pack to his right eye when Caroline entered the kitchen awhile later dressed in jeans and a green polo. The fit of her jeans showed off her slim shape. But it wasn't her figure that held Jack's notice. His attention had stalled on her wild-looking, zebra-striped hair.

Totally distracted, Caroline pulled open a cabinet to search for the telephone book. She'd blow-dried her hair. If anything, it had made it look even worse. The only TV role she was perfectly cast for now, she'd decided, was an alien from outer space, and there wasn't a soap opera with Mars as its locale. And if enough wasn't enough, she didn't need Jack Corey staring at her. Caroline shifted a glance his way and found him looking like he was about to laugh. She couldn't believe it! Did he still think this was funny? And where was his shirt? He was sitting at her table with just his undershirt on.

Myra came into the kitchen from the utility room with Jack's blue denim work shirt now warm and toasty from the dryer. He'd declined her offer to toss in his jeans. Myra handed Jack his shirt, and then while he put it on she looked over at Caroline. "My, God!" Myra's expression was one of shock. "Caroline, what have you done to your hair?"

Before Caroline had the chance to answer, Bobby and Elizabeth came running into the kitchen.

"Mom, you look like a weirdo," Bobby said, offering his comment as he and his sister circled around her.

"No, she doesn't," Elizabeth said excitedly. "She looks like Madonna." Elizabeth was fixated on anything that at all resembled the singer. "Is it a wig, Mommy? Can I wear it?"

"It's not a wig." Caroline's bottom lip trembled. "I can't believe I've done this to myself."

Poor kid, Jack thought before he gave himself a mental kick. He was becoming far too absorbed in her predicaments, losing sight of his own. How could he have ever described her as cool and calm? She was a walking disaster.

Myra shook her head in dismay. "You are going to have to get yourself to a beautician."

Caroline chewed the corner of her mouth. "I know. That's why I need the phone book. I've got to find a beauty parlor. Where did we put the phone book?" She was making a concerted effort not to look over at Jack, but she could feel his eyes on her—his one eye, anyway. And she was furious at him because she was embarrassed. For two cents she would have slugged him again, and this time she would have meant it.

"It's Sunday," Myra said, pointing out the obvious as she located the phone book and handed it to Caroline. "I don't think there's going to be a beauty parlor open today."

Jack put the ice pack down again. He really did feel for her. She was in a jam. Not that he wasn't in a jam himself. But there was nothing he could do about his own problems at the moment. And there was something he could do about hers.

He got up and walked over to her. She was walking her fingers down the list of beauty parlors in the Yellow Pages.

"I know a beautician who can do your hair today," he said. "I'll take you there."

Her eyes flew up to his face. "Are you serious?"

Jack nodded his head.

Caroline gave him a wide-eyed, grateful look. Her impulse was to throw her arms around his neck and thank him for rescuing her. "You're being very nice," she said, ashamed of the names she'd been thinking up for him in her head.

Jack smiled. "You needn't look so surprised."

"You don't have to take me there. Just give me the name of the place and I'll phone for an appointment. I don't want to put you out."

Jack grinned. "Put me out? You've got to be kidding. I feel like I've already been through a war with you."

Caroline laughed.

Jack found himself thinking she had a very nice laugh. Then he quickly remembered that he'd once thought is ex-fiancé had a very nice laugh.... Women! Why did they all come packed with so much ammunition?

"Let's go," he practically barked.

Caroline was taken aback by his sharp tone. "I just need to get my purse."

"But, Mommy," Bobby complained, swallowing down the cookie he'd been eating while watching the adults. "You said you would take us to the beach. You promised."

"I know I did...." Caroline faltered, upset at having to break a promise to her kids.

Myra stepped in. "I'll take you both to the beach. And if the two of you are good, I'll take you out for dinner tonight."

"We want to go to McDonald's," Bobby negotiated with his sister's approval. Elizabeth was too busy chewing her second chocolate chip cookie to open her mouth.

"Okay," Myra agreed and waved Caroline off.

Caroline gave her kids big hugs and then issued an order that they were not to have any more cookies. She thanked Myra profusely, grabbed her handbag and noticed Bobby's Mets baseball cap on the counter. She grabbed it and left the house with Jack.

In the bright daylight Caroline could see that the area around Jack's right eye was already turning black and blue. Jack caught Caroline's concerned look as they walked toward his car.

"Does it hurt?" she asked.

"Don't worry." He stopped walking to face her. "This isn't the first time I've had a shiner, but it is a record one. I've never gotten one from a woman before."

"This is a first for me, too. I've never given anyone a shiner before." Their eyes met and held for a moment. Caroline was certain the bruise had to hurt, but it didn't detract any from his sexy charisma. The guy had a lot of charisma.

They broke eye contact at about the same moment, and then they both hurried to Jack's car.

Jack slipped on a pair of sunglasses after he'd turned the motor over. Caroline popped the Mets cap on her head, tucked her damaged hair under it, and then settled back into the seat beside him.

They drove in silence for several minutes. Jack glanced over at her. "So, slugger, why did they cut you from the soap? I thought you were good."

She gave him a surprised look. "You saw me on the show?"

"Only once. I'm not a big soap fan. Football's more my thing. But I was curious. And like I said, I thought you were good."

"I got killed," Caroline answered, turning her head his way. His jeans looked like they'd been ironed to his thighs, having dried that way after the hosing Bobby had given him earlier. She redirected her gaze.

"Could you flash that by me again? What do you mean you got killed?"

"The writers killed my character on the show. Of course, the episode hasn't aired yet, but when the bank checked for final approval, they were told. But don't worry. I have two auditions set up for tomorrow on two other soaps, and the bank assured me that if I got another part they'd be able to close on the house within a few days." She didn't consider that a lie. She'd just stretched the truth a bit, and it was possible that the bank would comply.

"What if you don't get another part right away?"

"I will." Caroline said with determined self-confidence.

"Have you ever thought of trying a different line of work?" Jack suggested.

"I did work with my ex-husband for years helping him build up his coin dealership business. But I've never liked business. I had planned to make a career in acting before I met Steve. Now I've made up my mind to give it my all. Besides, I can't think of any other career that pays as well. And money is an issue."

When wasn't money an issue? Jack wondered to himself, feeling some annoyance with her remark.

"Is this soap the first acting you've done?" he asked, addressing her a bit coolly. Maybe he should have said *paid* acting... women were born actresses.

Reacting to his tone, Caroline felt a little huffy. "I got my first part right after I graduated high school in an off-Broadway show. Well, off-off-Broadway," she qualified, not wanting to lie. "I did a few more shows...again, off-off-Broadway, and then I got married. After that, I kept my career down to a minimum. I did commercials now and then. That was about it. I'm going to do better now."

"It's not very steady work," Jack remarked.

"Tell me about it..." Caroline sighed. "I thought I'd grabbed the brass ring when I landed the role on 'Days to Remember.'"

Jack decided he was sounding like Nina when she gave him lectures on how to live his life. "Sorry. It's none of my business." Well, that wasn't altogether true. "So, what kind of parts are you trying out for?"

"One is a woman who's supposed to look like the typical girl next door—sort of nondescript—and turns out to be a secret agent for an underground network of spies."

Her hair aside, he still wouldn't have called her nondescript. "Is she on the side of law and order?" he asked, warming to the topic as he pictured her in the role.

Caroline tossed Jack an impish look. "You'll have to tune in to find out."

"I see," Jack said, smiling. "What about the other part?" His eyes traveled to the baseball cap perched on her zebra-striped hair. At the moment, she'd be perfect as a punk rocker.

"The other part's a woman who's had amnesia for the last ten years. After a car accident, she's brought to a hospital where one of the doctors realizes that she's the long-lost daughter of a dying millionaire."

"How does he realize that?"

"The doctor who treats her is the same doctor who treated her when she was in her teens, and he recognizes a very distinctive birthmark on her body."

"Where's the birthmark?"

"I wasn't told, but all the writers that I've come across have very vivid imaginations." Caroline exchanged a look with Jack—his was amused, hers was saucy.

"Does the millionaire die?" He fixed his attention back on the expressway.

"Of course, and she becomes an heiress and gets wooed by the handsome, sexy, ne'er-do-well on the show who wants to romance himself into a fortune. It sets up a number of steamy love scenes, which is what keeps the ratings up."

Jack sent her a look. "Just how steamy do those love scenes get?"

"Very steamy," Caroline quipped, fanning her face with her hand to punctuate her point.

"Uh-huh." Jack's mouth quirked into a grin. Then an image of her in a steamy love scene took hold of his thoughts and wouldn't let go. "It must be kind of awkward doing those scenes. All those people watching. How do you...uh...keep from getting personally involved?" He could feel his cheeks heat up. It wasn't like him to blush.

"It's called acting," Caroline answered a little archly. But then she laughed. "The rehearsals before taping can drag on forever. I usually spend the time thinking up my shopping list and planning out meals for the week."

Jack laughed, too. But underneath he was a little irked with himself. What possible difference did it make to him what she felt during those steamy love scenes?

Caroline shrugged. "Anyway, I think I've got a better chance of landing the girl-next-door role than the part of the billionaire temptress."

"Why do you say that?"

Why had she said that? It was a dumb thing to say when she was trying to assure him that she had all these opportunities at landing a new part and getting a mortgage.

"Look," she began, "I want you to know that I wouldn't have committed myself to buying the house if I'd had any idea I was going to be written out of the show. They kept assuring me that I was going to get a new and ongoing story line. I couldn't believe it when I got that pink slip instead of a five-year contract."

Jack glanced in his side-view mirror before switching lanes. "What made them change their minds?"

"They said there wasn't any...chemistry between myself and the actor that they had me playing opposite. They said they'd been waiting for the screen to ignite, but it never happened."

"Ignite?"

"I mean attraction. A guy is attracted to a woman. A woman is attracted to a guy. And even if they don't want to fall for each other, they can't help themselves. The audience has to be able to see and feel that—that's what ignites the screen—and that's what keeps the audience interested in all the complications."

"The complications?" He was having trouble following her.

"You know, complications. What would a romance be without complications? Soaps are supposed to imitate life."

"Is that how you see romance, full of complications?"

"Personally, I've had it with romance. Love doesn't last. It's all just an illusion."

He had no trouble understanding her now...she'd just spouted off his own philosophy. "What about attraction?" he asked, his masculine interest sparked. "How do you handle that?"

"It's easy enough to handle on a set. You just remind yourself it's make-believe."

"And off the set?"

Caroline gave him a quick look. "Let's just say that I don't trust attraction."

"You mean you don't trust men," he corrected her, remembering her earlier tirade.

"Let's say I just stopped believing in fairy tales."

"Cinderella home from the ball, huh?" His tone was soft. He guessed she was referring to her failed marriage. He recalled her heated remark about how men were quick to dump one woman for another. Had her husband dumped her for another woman? Is that why they were divorced?

"I've never quite thought of myself as a Cinderella."

"Maybe that's because the right Prince Charming hasn't come along." Now why had he said that? It sounded like a come-on line.

"With my luck, he'll turn into a frog." She laughed.

He laughed with her.

The laughter was quickly followed by an awkward silence. Jack's foot pressed down harder on the accelerator.

Caroline suggested he slow down, which reminded Jack that he was still driving without his license, and he'd already gotten one ticket today. That reminded him of the whole crazy sequence of events that had followed, which brought him full circle back to his problem.

He slowed down and turned his head slightly to bring her into his vision. "About the closing..."

"I'm sure to land a part."

"Since you seem so sure, maybe you've got a friend in the business or someone in your family who could cosign..."

"I wouldn't feel comfortable asking a friend. And my folks live on my dad's small pension from teaching. It would be pressure for them, and I don't want them worrying about me and the kids."

"Well, what about your husband? I mean... your ex-husband? Wouldn't he want to help you out in a situation like this? For the kids?"

"Forget it, Jack. No way," Caroline said tersely.

"Not an amicable divorce?"

She laughed sharply. "I've heard of them, but I've never known anyone to actually have one, myself included."

She hadn't wanted the divorce in the first place. She'd wanted to keep on trying, even if it was just for the kids. But Steve wanted out. For one thing, he'd said her minor disasters drove him crazy. He wanted order in his life. Well, she'd wanted romance. Stupidly, she'd thought romance was supposed to be part of marriage.

Caroline sighed inwardly and pulled the baseball cap down tighter. Why was there always a minor disaster waiting around every corner she turned?

"How long have you been divorced?"

"Eight months." In retrospect, Caroline realized that she and Steve had been wrong for each other right from the beginning. Other than attraction, they'd had nothing in common. She'd always been a die-hard romantic and artsy. Steve was the staid, proper businessman type who preplanned every step of his life.

"Are you dating?" Jack asked.

"No." She wasn't even thinking in that direction. But if and when she did start dating, she was going to steer clear of businessmen.

In an attempt to end this conversation, Caroline reached out and turned the car radio on. The dial was already preset to a Spanish music station.

Jack took the hint and stopped his questions. Obviously, she didn't want to talk about her personal life. Well, neither did he.

Restlessly, he drummed out the beat to the music with his fingers on the wheel.

Even with the music, Jack found the silence between them uncomfortable. "You didn't tell me why you don't think you'll get the part of the billionaire temptress?"

"For one thing, I doubt they they want a temptress who looks like she got her hair caught in a mixmaster."

"Don't worry about your hair. We'll get it fixed." Jack reached across and gave her hand a reassuring squeeze. He had an uneasy feeling that he'd just jumped on an excuse to touch her.

Caroline quickly pulled her hand out from under his, even though she'd liked the support he'd offered. "It's not just my hair."

"Then what is it?" He put both his hands back on the wheel.

"I just don't have the right look. I'm not the temptress type, and so I don't get the bad-girl roles that are really the best roles on the soaps. They're the only ones that have any stability, and stability is really what I'm after. I mean, I have two kids to bring up, and that's why I bought the house. Kids need a home, a backyard, a dog, a garden..."

He agreed with her that children needed a home, security, a place to feel was theirs. He thought back to his own childhood. His father had walked out on his mother when he was five years old. She had struggled to make ends meet, but it had been tough. They must have lived in a dozen apartments before he was fifteen. And then she died...

"What are you thinking about?" Caroline broke into his thoughts.

Jack had almost forgotten she was there. "Oh... nothing. Just that a home is important to kids."

Caroline felt a fluttering of hope. Maybe Jack would hold off selling the house to someone else and give her a little more time.

"Right." Her gaze stayed on his profile, and she was flustered to find herself thinking about the warm, personal feel of the kiss he'd planted on her cheek. She was suddenly acutely conscious of his rakish masculinity.

"What are you thinking about?" It was Jack's turn to ask.

Caroline felt her cheeks warm. "I—I was just wondering how much farther it is to the beauty parlor."

"Not far," Jack answered, slanting his head her way. His gaze lingered a little long. The honk of a nearby horn made him quickly redirect his attention to the road. Then he had to weave sharply in front of the car to his right. He'd been so busy looking at her, he'd nearly missed the exit.

Chapter Three

Jack was looking out for a parking space. Caroline was just looking around. The streets were lined with small apartment houses and a mix of retail establishments. She spotted a Spanish grocery store and a sign in the window of a children's clothing shop that proclaimed, *Se Habla Español.* They drove past a group of dark-haired teenaged boys in denim jackets sitting on a stoop with a couple of girls.

"This beautician must be really good if you go out of your way like this to get your hair cut," Caroline commented. She knew Jack didn't live too far from the house that wasn't quite hers yet. "She does cut your hair, too, right?"

Jack nodded his head as he spied a Camaro pulling out further down the street. He pressed his foot against the accelerator and raced to claim the space.

Caroline could see the beauty parlor now. She could also see that it was closed. "It figures," she muttered.

"What figures?" Jack asked while he expertly straightened out his Toyota up against the curb with one easy swing.

"The place is closed."

"Don't worry. The lady who owns it lives right upstairs, and I have a special relationship with her." Jack turned the motor off. "I guarantee you that she'll open the place and do your hair."

Caroline deduced from his remark that the lady upstairs was more than just his beautician.

"Great," she said, forcing a smile. She didn't know why it would matter, but she was not particularly thrilled to be meeting his girlfriend.

Jack got out of the car. Caroline knew he was coming around to open the door for her, but she didn't wait for him. She opened the passenger door herself and stepped out onto the street.

"It's the second floor," Jack said as they walked to the door of the three-story building.

Caroline nodded. She wondered how long they'd been going out? She wondered if the relationship was serious? She wondered what she was doing wondering so much about him?

Jack held the door open to the apartment side of the building, which was just to the side of the beauty parlor. He caught a flicker of agitation in Caroline's eyes as she passed him. "This is a nice, safe, working-class neighborhood. Relax."

"I'm not worried about the neighborhood. Back when I was doing off-Broadway..."

"You mean off-off-Broadway," he teased.

"Right. Anyway, I shared an apartment not far from here. There's a great Spanish restaurant right down the street."

"You like Spanish food?"

"I love Spanish food."

They came to the staircase. Again the look of apprehension shadowed Caroline's face.

"If it's not the neighborhood, what is it?" he questioned as they started up the first flight of stairs.

"What do you mean?" She was supposed to be an actress. Why, all of a sudden, couldn't she put on a better show?

"You seem angry."

"Why would I be angry? I'm just worried that your girlfriend might not be able to fix my hair."

Jack stopped walking and leaned back against the iron banister. Caroline had no choice but to stop on the stair with him.

"What makes you think she's my girlfriend?"

"I just assumed. Isn't she?" Caroline fiddled with her shoulder bag and then with the brim of her baseball cap. She was suddenly very fidgety.

"Does it make a difference?" He lifted his sunglasses, observing her flushed cheeks.

His observation only made her cheeks rosier. "Of course not! It's just..." Stuck for an excuse, she didn't finish.

"What?" A smile worked on his features. He liked the way she blushed.

"There are things about me that you don't know," Caroline began, struggling to finesse herself out of this situation. She certainly didn't want to give him the impression that she was interested in him. She wasn't interested in him, she assured herself. She was just...irritated.

"There's a lot about you that I don't know," Jack said, filling in the pause. Which was exactly the way he wanted it... or was it?

"What I'm trying to say, is that I don't feel right taking advantage of...of your relationship with...this woman. I mean, it's Sunday and she may not want..."

"I won't have any trouble persuading her to do me a favor." Jack flipped up the brim of Caroline's baseball cap. He wanted to see her eyes.

Caroline's eyes narrowed before she flipped the brim back down. "I'm sure you're very good at persuading women to do your bidding."

Jack couldn't help laughing.

"I don't see any reason for you to be entertained." She gave him a "drop dead" look. "Just how do you intend to explain your black eye?"

Jack flicked his sunglasses back down over his eyes. "I'll keep these on. If Nina sees my eye she'll go wild, thinking I got into a brawl."

Caroline remembered him saying this wasn't his first shiner. "Do you get into brawls often?" Her tone was a bit patronizing.

Jack grinned. "Not since I was a teenager. But Nina has a long memory."

Oh, Caroline thought with annoyance, childhood sweethearts, no less.

A young woman carrying a small baby started down the stairs. Caroline flattened herself up against the wall to make room.

The woman stopped as she noticed Jack. *"Cómo está usted, Jack?"*

"Bien," Jack answered and looked at the baby. *"Grande...muy grande."*

Caroline peeked at the baby and then looked across at Jack. "How do you say 'beautiful' in Spanish?" she asked him, smiling softly with her eyes all bright. She loved babies.

"*Bonito,*" he answered, trying to find a place to set his gaze other than on Caroline, but his screened eyes kept coming back to her as she cooed at the baby and then smiled at him. That smile of hers was quite disarming.

"Is it a girl or a boy?" Caroline asked.

"A *muchacho*—a boy," the young mother answered proudly, and then after giving both Caroline and Jack a happy look, she continued down the stairs.

They were alone again and staring at each other. At least she was staring at him. She couldn't quite tell where his eyes were with his sunglasses on. Caroline cleared her throat. "You seem to know more than one person in this building. I guess you come here quite often."

"Yes," Jack responded, walking with her up the stairs. "I also lived here for a while."

She couldn't believe this! This guy was so cocky, he kept his women on a string even after he was halfway through with them.... Her irritation was skyrocketing as he knocked on the door to 2B.

Nine saw Jack first as she opened the door. Caroline had stepped behind him. "What are you doing here? You didn't say you were coming." Nina smiled. "Gloria and Ray are here, too."

"Good. I need to speak to Ray." Jack reached back for Caroline's head and pulled her forward as he stepped in. "First, I want you to meet someone."

Caroline's mouth dropped open as she looked at Nina. This woman did not look anything at all like she'd imagined. She was attractive, but she was much too old for Jack....

"Caroline Phelps," Jack said, making the introductions, "this is Nina Sanchez. Momma, meet Caroline."

"Momma...?" Caroline murmured.

"Ever since he was fifteen." Nina smiled. "I'm so happy Jack brought you over. I wish I had something on the stove, but I can put something together very quickly."

Nina ushered her through the foyer, Jack following. "Wait until Gloria sees you. She's a big fan of 'Days to Remember,' too. Now that she's working days, she tapes the show so she can see it at night."

"Where are Gloria and Ray?" Jack asked.

"In the kitchen. Come on." Nina hurried. "I've got some rice and beans in the fridge, and I could cook up some chicken...." She was scurrying ahead of them down the hall to the kitchen.

"Momma, huh?" Caroline whispered to Jack.

"Next time, don't jump to such a quick conclusion," Jack whispered back playfully as they walked after Nina.

"You led me on deliberately," Caroline rebutted.

"Gloria, look who's here," Nina said, excited. "It's Gabrielle Fallon. I should say, Caroline Phelps, the actress."

Gloria Aranez got up from her seat at the table. She was petite and pretty with long, wavy ebony hair. Her white slacks and pink jersey top complemented her honey complexion.

"You *are* Gabrielle Fallon," Gloria confirmed, looking closer at Caroline, thinking the baseball cap she had on was an effective disguise. "Hey, Jack, you never told me you knew any TV stars," she teased. Then she focused back on Caroline. "I can't believe you're here. A soap opera star in this kitchen."

Caroline gave Jack a wan look. Make that ex-soap opera would-be star.

"You've got to tell us what's going to happen next on the show. Are you starting to fall in love with Arty Devon?" Gloria rushed on.

"Well," Caroline started to speak when Nina interrupted.

"She's too smart to fall in love with someone like Arty Devon."

"Hey, don't I get introduced?" Ray asked, standing next to Gloria.

"Ray," Jack said, "this is Caroline Phelps."

Ray shook hands with Caroline, and Jack said, "Caroline, this is Nina's son, Ray Sanchez."

Ray, a tanned, rugged-looking young man with dark eyes and hair the color of India ink, smiled warmly at Caroline and then winked at Jack. "Hey, bro'. Your taste's improving."

Jack and Caroline flushed in unison.

"Let's sit down. We'll all have coffee and then I'll cook up something to eat," Nina said.

Caroline looked over at Jack, signaling him to explain that the reason for their visit wasn't a meal, but Jack shrugged.

Nina was getting two more cups and saucers while Gloria and Ray and Jack and finally Caroline sat down. The round white Formica table and stainless steel chairs with orange vinyl seat cushions accommodated six.

Caroline glanced around. Overhead, a white ceramic fixture added more light to the room than did a small window looking into an alley. Floral wallpaper further encouraged brightness.

Caroline drew an image of Jack at fifteen when he'd first come to live here. She wondered what had become of his natural parents. Had he been too incorrigible for his folks to manage? Caroline couldn't believe that. Jack Corey didn't strike her as the type to look for trouble, just the type who wouldn't turn his back on it if trouble found him.

"Who's Arty Devon?" Ray asked, looking from Caroline to Gloria.

"He's a guy on the soap," Gloria answered. "Gabrielle doesn't know it, but he's the one who framed her father and sent him to jail. Now she's working a second job at night as a waitress to pay back the money her father was accused of stealing. Caroline, how long is it going to take before you figure out what Arty Devon is really like?"

"I think you just told her," Ray said, exchanging a grin with Jack.

"Don't make fun of me." Gloria rebuffed Ray with pretended chagrin. "You know that I take the soaps seriously. And Jack, I think you can take your sunglasses off in the house."

Nina agreed, calling to Jack over her shoulder. "It's bad for your eyes to wear sunglasses in the house."

Jack gave Caroline a *what can I do* look as he took them off and twirled them in his hand.

Caroline sank down in her seat while Ray and Gloria fixed their attention on Jack's shiner. He wasn't going to tell them every detail leading up to his black-and-blue eye, was he? Yes, he probably was, she decided, and thought of kicking him under the table.

"That's a beaut." Ray grinned. *"Qué pasó?"*

"Caroline decked me," Jack responded with a broad smile. Caroline could see that he was obviously enjoying himself.

"What did you do to deserve it?" Nina asked reproachfully, as she walked over to the table with two more cups of coffee—one for Caroline and one for Jack.

Caroline had to laugh at Nina's immediate assumption that Jack had been at fault. "It was an accident," Caroline hastened to explain as Nina took a seat. "Jack, tell him how it happened."

"You want me to tell them what happened?" He had another teasing look on his face. "I'll tell them what happened.... She caught me off guard. Talk about giving a guy a fighting chance..."

Gloria scoffed. "What really happened?"

Caroline answered. "I was trying to stop Myra from hitting him over the head with her handbag, and I got him in the eye."

Jack grinned. "I don't know what it is that makes women want to attack me."

Gloria laughed. "Machismo, as if you didn't know."

Caroline once again felt her cheeks warm up. Machismo? Well, she couldn't argue with that.

"Who is Myra?" Nina asked. "And where did this happen?"

"It happened in Caroline's bathroom," Jack answered blithely.

Caroline felt six pairs of eyes turn to her. "It's not the way Jack is making it sound," she said quickly. "Myra is the woman who lives with me. And she misunderstood what Jack and I were doing on the floor in the bathroom...." She stopped, realizing she was only making it worse.

"What were you doing on the floor? In the bathroom?" Gloria asked, looking from Caroline to Jack and then back to Caroline. This was better than the soaps.

"We...slipped. There was shampoo...on the floor." Caroline tried to explain. Then, with all eyes on her, she pulled off her baseball cap, giving everyone new reason to stare at her.

"Jack, did you do that to her hair?" Nina questioned in alarm.

"No, he didn't do it." Caroline threw up her hand. "I did it."

"For your part on the soap?" Gloria asked ingenuously.

"No, it wasn't supposed to look like this. I left the solution on too long. I... fell asleep. If Jack hadn't shown up at my door, it might have been even... worse." If worse was possible. She was mortified when she felt tears stinging her eyes. How could she break down and cry in front of all these strangers?

Nina gave her a comforting pat on her back. "I've fixed plenty worse dye jobs in my day. This is nothing. First, I'm going to give you an oil treatment, and then clip a little, then use a nice, soft rinse...."

Caroline swallowed hard as she got to her feet. "How much will you have to cut off?" She was picturing herself in a crew cut. Why was it that when things were going bad, they only got worse?

"I'll have to see. Don't worry. With a pretty face like yours..." She stopped. "But the soap... The writers will have a job coming up with a reason why you cut your hair off."

"Cut it... off?" Caroline echoed mordantly.

Gloria piped in with, "I've got an idea why Gabrielle would cut her hair. I'll go down to the beauty parlor with you and we can talk about it. Maybe the writers will like it."

"Good," Nina said.

"Caroline," Jack called to her as she started to leave the kitchen with Nina and Gloria.

"What?" Caroline swiveled to face him.

"I just want you to know that I think you're going to look great with short hair." He smiled at her, wanting her to feel better.

"Oh," Caroline said and smiled back, thanking him even more with her eyes. Then she left with Nina and Gloria.

"Well, well, well," Ray said as he heard the front door close.

"Well, well, well, yourself," Jack returned. "And what's that supposed to mean?"

"Nothing." Ray rolled his eyes. "I like her. That's all."

"You're spoken for."

"You're not." Ray grinned.

"And that's the way I like it," Jack countered. "I'm not ready to have another woman mess up my life. What am I saying? This one's already messed me up."

Ray laughed. "You know what Momma says. After a fight, the best thing to do is kiss and make up."

"Very funny." Jack scowled. "Maybe you can think up something funny for me to tell Taylor that will get us an extension."

"What do we need an extension for? You're going to have the closing tomorrow. Right?"

"Wrong. Gabrielle is dead."

"Gabrielle? What are you talking about?"

"Caroline's soap character. Dead. *Muerta.*"

"You mean she's been axed? Fired?"

"Ah, the light dawns," Jack quipped, but he eyed Ray with a downcast gaze.

"Did you tell Caroline that you needed the money to go into a business deal?"

"No, and I don't want you to say anything. She's feeling lousy enough as it is."

"I know how lousy feels," Ray said. "I feel lousy that I haven't got any money to contribute. It's not fair, you putting in all the start-up funds."

"You're going to put in your share of muscle."

"Look, Jack, I know you're doing this as much for me as for you. Don't you think it's time that I stood on my own two feet again? You don't have to keep your eye on me anymore. I'm through throwing away everything I make on the ponies."

"It's a good thing Gloria reformed you, because you couldn't pick a winner at the track if there was only one horse in the race."

"Yeah, yeah, yeah." Ray grinned. "Did I tell you that Phil Murray offered me a job?"

"What? You want to be a used-car salesman?"

"I'm pretty good with my mouth, and what's wrong with selling used cars?"

"Nothing. I just want you to be my partner, that's all."

"Then why don't we keep working the way we have been? Let me put part of my salary back into the business and let's climb to the top on our own. We'll do okay."

"I want to do better than okay, and Taylor's deal is our ticket to success, Ray."

"Hey, Jack, just because Jill walked out on you for some rich jerk doesn't mean you have to prove something."

"I'm not out to prove anything. My ego may still be a little bent out of shape, but my head is on straight."

"What happens if you can't talk Taylor into giving you more time?"

"I'll cross that bridge when I come to it," Jack answered, going over to the phone.

Caroline came out from under the hair dryer as Nina raised the hood.

"The oil treatment helped," Nina said, fingering Caroline's greasy hair. "Now, let's get it washed."

"I'm really mad that you're not going to be on 'Days to Remember' anymore," Gloria said, following Nina and Caroline to the back of the shop. "I'm going to stop watching it."

"Thanks for feeling that way," Caroline said, smiling. She'd confided in both women that she'd lost her job and her mortgage commitment. "But you shouldn't stop watching it. It is a good soap."

"You could come back to the show as your twin," Nina said encouragingly as she motioned to Caroline to sit down in front of the middle sink.

"I could if they wanted me, but they don't," Caroline said, with a sigh, then sat down and leaned back.

Nina turned on both faucets and tested the water coming out of the spray. "Jack must have been very disappointed that he's not going to have the money to get into that building deal."

"What building deal?" Caroline asked.

"Didn't he tell you what he needed the money from the closing for?" Nina questioned.

Caroline shook her head as Nina wet her hair. "No, he didn't say anything. No wonder he's so upset. I didn't realize he had immediate plans for the money. I feel terrible."

"It's not your fault," Gloria said. "Jack didn't have immediate plans until a few weeks ago. Anyway, I don't think Ray really wants to get in on the deal."

"Oh," Caroline groaned. "Are you saying that I've thrown a monkey wrench into both their plans?"

"Jack shouldn't have bought that house for her to begin with," Nina said, looking over Caroline's head at Gloria. "I knew *she* wouldn't like it."

"Who did he buy the house for?" Caroline asked while Nina scrubbed her hair with shampoo.

"That little gold digger he foolishly got himself engaged to," Nina answered. "I am glad it's over and done with."

"I just hope he's not carrying a torch for her," Gloria mused.

"After the way she treated him," Nina exclaimed. "He better not be carrying a torch."

Caroline felt a rush of compassion for Jack. No wonder he was down on women. "What happened between them?" she asked.

Gloria replied, "She gave him back his ring a week before they were supposed to get married. She told him that she'd suddenly realized that she was still in love with an old boyfriend—a rich old boyfriend," Gloria elaborated expressively. "Jill has very expensive taste."

Caroline sat up. "How long ago did this happen?"

"Six months ago," Gloria answered. "He denies it, but I think he's still licking his wounds. She really did a number on him."

"Come sit in the front," Nina said to Caroline. "I'll see how much I have to cut, and then I'm going to blend some color back into your hair."

Caroline's mind was not on her hair. "What kind of a woman would string a guy along like that? That's really rotten! I just can't believe..."

Nina interrupted. "Caroline, what size shoes do you wear?"

Caroline blinked. "What?"

Nina repeated her question.

"A size six...sometimes a six and a half," Caroline answered, wondering if Nina was in the shoe business on the side.

"Boy, your feet are almost as small as mine," Gloria remarked.

Nina just smiled.

Jack took a look at his watch for the umpteenth time. He was sitting with Ray in the living room in front of the TV watching a baseball game. "How much longer do you think they're going to be? It's almost two hours since they went downstairs."

Ray shifted his attention from the TV to look over at Jack. "Quit being so edgy. What are you worried about now? You were great on the phone with Taylor. We got the extension, didn't we? It's a good thing he's having some problems on his end."

"I'm not edgy."

"If you're not edgy about business, then maybe Caroline's got you in a state. You are edgy."

"I'm not edgy and I'm not in any state. Why would she have me edgy?"

Ray grinned. "Maybe you go for gals with striped hair."

"I assure you that I'm not in the least bit attracted to her. But I guess I am worried about her hair. Appearances are important in her line of work, and if she doesn't get another part quick I'm going to be sunk. Taylor should have his end worked out in a couple of weeks."

Ray's grin widened. "Momma will get her hair fixed. But I have a ten-spot sitting in my pocket that says Caroline will still have you edgy."

The front door opened. Jack shot up from the couch and walked into the hall. Ray followed at his heels. He wasn't going to miss this.

Nina walked in first, followed by Gloria and then Caroline.

Jack was prepared to tell Caroline she looked good even if Nina hadn't been able to do much with her hair.

"Isn't anybody going to say anything?" Nina asked, looking at Jack who was looking at Caroline.

Caroline was holding her breath as she stood center stage waiting for Jack's response.

Jack couldn't seem to come up with the right words, or *any* words as he concentrated on Caroline. Her hair was blended just a shade lighter than her own natural color to a tawny dark blond. Nina had cut it short—boyishly short. It gave Caroline a new look—sexier and sophisticated, but still soft and feminine. And her sparkling hazel eyes really stood out.

"Wow," Ray said finally.

Jack nodded his head. Wow just about summed it up. So why was he feeling edgier than ever?

Chapter Four

"Hold it a second," Jack said. "I don't think I've got this straight. Did she marry Tom's son Bill before she'd divorced and married Tom and after she'd married and divorced Tom's father?"

"She never married Tom's father," Caroline explained. "He was just one of her lovers. But there was some question as to whether Tom's brother might not have also been Tom's nephew."

Jack flashed a quick smile, trying to get that digested.

Ray checked his watch. "Gloria, we'd better get going if we're going to get to your parents on time for dinner. Let's keep in mind that they're still debating whether or not they approve of me."

Gloria sent Ray a warm smile. They'd all been sitting in Nina's living room for about an hour, chatting away. Nina, Gloria and Caroline had been talking about the soaps and their convoluted story lines. Jack and Ray had been laughing heartily and offering some of their own suggestions for plot twists.

Gloria got to her feet. "I guess we'd better get going."

Everyone stood up. Gloria hugged Nina, and then she hugged Caroline. Ray elbowed Jack in the ribs, and cocked his head toward Caroline. "Don't let her get away," Ray jived, dropping his voice so only Jack would hear him.

Jack glowered at him, but he wasn't actually annoyed. The two men good-naturedly ribbed each other at any opportunity.

"I really enjoyed meeting you," Caroline said a second later as Ray gave her a quick bear hug.

"I just know we're all going to see a lot more of each other." Ray smiled at Caroline and then Jack.

Nina walked to the door with Gloria and Ray. Caroline and Jack took their seats again. Jack sat in one of the two green-on-green patterned armchairs, legs stretched out, fingers linked across his hard abdomen. He looked nonchalant. Inside, he was antsy again.

Caroline sat on the paisley print couch. For no particular reason, she felt suddenly awkward being alone in the room with Jack. She did know that he was watching her, even though her eyes were focused on the hands she'd folded in her lap. She wondered if his bruise still hurt? She'd noticed that his jeans looked more comfortable now that he'd moved in them for a while.

Jack wanted to say something, if only to break the quiet. "So, she did marry all those guys?"

"Yes." Caroline nodded.

He smiled at her. "You really look great."

To Caroline's surprise her heart picked up speed and went pitter-patter in overdrive. Why was she putting so much stock in his assessment? "Really?" Her eyes met his, and her fingers went to her hair. He hadn't actually voiced his opinion until now.

"Really." His tone was easier.

Nina came back into the room. She glanced at Caroline. She glanced at Jack.

Caroline got up from the couch. "I can't thank you enough for helping me out with my hair," she told Nina again. "I don't know what I would have done."

"It was my pleasure." Nina smiled, thinking she'd invite the two of them to stay for dinner, but then she came up with a much better matchmaking scheme. "The two of you must be hungry." She gave Jack an all-too-guileless look. "Why don't you take Caroline out for something to eat?"

Jack hesitated on his way to picking up the ball. It wasn't that he had any real objection to taking Caroline for something to eat. He just knew what Nina was up to.

Caroline quickly filled in, what was for her, an embarrassing pause. She certainly didn't need Jack to be coerced into going out with her for something to eat. Thank you!

"I should be getting home." Caroline directed herself to Nina. "I have the kids to make dinner for and I..."

"Myra has probably taken them to McDonald's already." Jack sprung to his feet. Knowing Nina as he did, five more minutes and she'd have his teenage picture album out. "Why don't we just go for a bite to eat?"

Caroline shot Jack a fast look. She was giving him an easy out. What was his problem? "Right, but I still have a lot more practice to do to get into character for my auditions tomorrow."

"It's early," Nina cajoled. "You'll still have plenty of time to practice after dinner. You have to eat."

"I'm not really hungry," Caroline responded. Of course, right then and there, her stomach pitched a fit and growled. She knew Jack heard it and her face flushed. Why did these things happen to her?

"I think that was my stomach talking." Jack winked. "Didn't you say there was a restaurant around here that you liked?"

"Yes. La Casa." Caroline was confused. Did he want to go out to eat with her?

"You're kidding...I know the family who owns the place. It's one of my favorite restaurants."

Nina, feeling pleased with her mission accomplished, prompted, "Then go and have a good time. I have things to do around here."

"Would it be all right if I used your phone to call home?" Caroline asked.

"Sure, in the kitchen," Nina replied.

As soon as Caroline left the room, Jack cornered Nina. "You can stop looking so smug. Nothing's going to come of trying to push us together."

Nina got indignant. "Who's pushing anybody? I'm not pushing anybody."

Jack gave her an all-too-knowing look. "I can see right through your little plan. Didn't I tell you not to try this with me?"

"You think you're so smart. You just behave yourself."

Jack groaned. "You behave yourself."

"She's a very nice girl," Nina pointed out, undaunted. "I wish you'd worn something different today. Comb your hair."

Humoring her, Jack ran a hand over his hair. He didn't carry a comb. Nina reached up and supplemented her professional touch. She straightened the collar of his blue denim shirt. Jack flipped it up after she'd finished. "Stop being so difficult," she scolded.

Jack grinned. "Look who's calling who difficult?"

Caroline came back into the living room. She'd let Myra know that she *might* be stopping for something to eat. Caroline was still debating the idea. She did remember to retrieve Bobby's baseball cap from the kitchen table.

"Ready?" Jack asked.

"Yes," Caroline answered.

Nina saw the two of them to the door. Caroline gave Nina a squeeze. Jack gave Nina a squeeze. Nina pinched Jack in the arm.

Going down the stairs, Jack said, "Okay if we walk to La Casa? It's less than a block away."

"Sure." Caroline didn't say anything else until they were out on the street. "Look, it's perfectly all right with me if you just take me home."

They stood in front of Nina's beauty parlor. It was still light enough at five-thirty for them to look each other in the face. Only Caroline had to tilt her head back to do so. She was five-foot-four in her flat sandals. He was over six feet tall.

"I'd rather take you to dinner," Jack said, actually meaning it. Somewhere in the last few minutes, he'd gotten used to the idea. Besides, he didn't have any other plans. "Of course, if you'd rather not, you needn't feel obliged to be polite."

Caroline took issue with him. She wasn't the one being polite here. "Hey wait a minute. Let's get the record straight. I'm not being polite. You're the one who is being polite."

Jack contemplated her. This was the nuttiest confrontation that had ever been directed his way. It took him a second before he comprehended where she was coming from. Then he realized she must have picked up on his initial reluctance. "It may not have looked like I wanted to take you to dinner at first. But that had nothing to do with you. It had to do with Nina."

"Nina?" Caroline didn't get it.

"I'll tell you on the way, if you go to dinner with me.... Of course, if you don't go to dinner with me, you don't get to know."

Caroline gave him a narrow look. But she was right at his side as he started walking, and they were moving toward the restaurant. She gave him sixty seconds to start talking. When he didn't, she pushed. "What about Nina?"

Jack considered stringing this out a bit, flirting with her. But he reconsidered. It wasn't a great idea. They were in a situation. She was pulling on her end. He was pulling on his. He wanted to help her out, but he didn't want to give her the impression that some friendliness on his part meant he was planning to be a chump.

"Nina was trying to fix us up. She's playing matchmaker. I just didn't want to encourage her."

Caroline was stunned. "Does she do that to you all the time?"

"No, you're her first target."

Caroline laughed.

Jack got a little uptight. "Hey, you're not going to give me a complex, are you?"

"I don't think you need fixing up." She estimated that any number of women would go bonkers over him. In fact, she had a sneaky suspicion that if she wanted to be perfectly honest with herself, she might concede that she wasn't entirely immune. But she wasn't looking to be perfectly honest with herself.

"You don't need fixing up, either." He smiled. "In my opinion, the role of the temptress is yours for the asking."

It was too much of a stretch for Caroline to see herself as a femme fatale. He was a charmer, though. There was no doubt about that.

"Thanks for the vote of confidence," she said lightly. "I hope the people I'm reading for tomorrow agree." It struck her suddenly that he had as much at stake as she had on tomorrow.

"What's wrong?" He was picking up on her body language. Not that it was hard. He'd spotted her crunching the baseball cap she was holding.

Caroline looked down. "I know I've put a crimp into your business deal."

Jack didn't have to figure hard to figure out how she knew. "Nina shouldn't have said anything to you. Don't worry about it. I called when you were downstairs, and there are some problems on the other end. The deal is off for a while."

"How long?"

"A while," Jack hedged.

"I'd rather you be honest with me."

"I am being honest. There isn't any immediate deadline. I give you my word that I'll always be honest with you." He delivered her a smile. "Okay?"

Caroline nodded, but she wasn't falling for any male-honesty routine. "This deal is very important to you, isn't it?"

"Yes. Just like being a famous soap opera star is important to you."

"Oh, I'm not into being famous. I just really like acting. I think it's a plus to work at something you really like."

"I thought you were into it for the chance to make big money." He remembered her making that remark earlier.

"Exactly. That's why I'm allowing myself to take this shot at it."

He didn't know if he had a handle on her. Was she chasing a dream or the almighty buck? "If you don't mind my asking, how are you going to manage between now and your next paycheck?"

"I'm okay on that end." She wanted to switch topics. This one was going to get around to him deciding she was not going to be able to buy the house. And she hadn't even given it her all yet.

He expected that her alimony was on that end, which was no skin off his nose.

Caroline saw La Casa's neon sign straight ahead. Jack quickened their pace. He opened the door when they got there, held it for her, and then followed her in.

La Casa was an old-fashioned neighborhood eatery with an embossed tin ceiling and a black-and-white ceramic floor. A long counter with stools dominated the front for the serious diners who weren't planning to make a night of it. The hangout crowd kept their vigil at the rear, where there were tables and booths, a postage-stamp-size wooden dance floor and a jukebox that played non-stop.

Caroline smiled, looking around, feeling nostalgic. The place looked the same as she remembered.

"Hey, Jack," shouted a balding, middle-aged man who was working busily behind the long counter. "Long time, no see." His greeting was echoed by a very pretty young woman with curly blond hair who was balancing four filled plates, two at the crooks of her elbows. She'd just come out of the kitchen door.

"Too long." Jack waved.

"There's plenty of room it the back," the waitress called over, passing out meals at the counter.

Jack placed a guiding hand on Caroline's elbow and ushered her toward the rear.

The group that usually congregated in the back didn't roll in until it turned dark out. Caroline and Jack had the pick of the place. She let him make the selection. He chose a booth near the dance floor. Caroline slid across one of the black vinyl benches, mended more than once with masking tape. Jack took the opposite bench. There were menus propped between the napkin holder and sugar bowl. Jack pulled out two and handed Caroline one.

He watched her study the single-sided, plastic-covered sheet after giving his a cursory glance.

"Would you like some help?" he asked finally, guessing she didn't read Spanish.

Caroline raised mischievously candid eyes. "I was going to try and bluff it. But I can't remember the name of the dish I used to order here all the time."

"Describe it to me."

Her mouth watered. "It was chicken with garlic sauce." Caroline almost changed her mind after she answered. But why shouldn't she order something with garlic? It wasn't like this was a date.

"Pollo Al Ajillo," Jack pronounced. "What would you like to drink?"

"A cola."

Jack took her menu, and along with his, put them back in place. They both listened to the Spanish ballad playing on the jukebox. The tune was slow and rhythmic. The tempo of the music hit him. He was tempted to ask her to dance, but he wasn't looking to be that sociable.

Caroline considered mentioning that this was going to be dutch. Then she decided there would be time enough to say so after they ate.

They both had their boundaries set. But neither thought of it that way.

The waitress who had greeted Jack came to the table. Caroline decided she was even prettier up close, guessing she was in her mid-twenties.

"How've you been, Sue?" Jack asked.

"Great." Sue gave him her full attention and noticed his shiner. "What kind of trouble have you been getting into?"

Jack smiled broadly. "Woman trouble, I guess." He pointed a finger at Caroline and said, "Sue Conway, this is Caroline Phelps."

Sue gave Caroline a second appraisal. "Did you give him that shiner?"

"Yes." Attacked by a moment of silliness, Caroline made a loose fist and blew across her fingernails. She looked at Jack. He was grinning. Caroline was pleased that he liked the way she was kidding around.

She laughed. "I guess next time he'll think twice before stepping out of line. Right, Jack?"

Jack gave Caroline a suggestive grin. It was his turn to play. "Either that, or next time I'll remember to hold her hands behind her back."

Caroline got the picture in her mind, and it brought a rosy tinge to her cheeks. She couldn't think of a comeback.

Sue was asking Jack, "What have you been doing with yourself? I haven't seen you in ages."

He hadn't seen much of any of his old friends in the past year that he'd been with Jill. He remembered bringing Jill here once, right after they'd met. She'd made it quite clear that La Casa was not to her liking, and neither were his friends.

"I'm sorry about . . ." Sue started, then caught herself in time.

"Yeah, well..." Jack was uncomfortable. He knew Sue had been about to bring up his broken engagement to Jill. "Are you and Eddie still seeing each other?"

"Yes, and we're still fighting." Sue chuckled. "What else is new?"

Jack smiled, sharing some history with Sue while Caroline looked on, aware that Sue had almost brought up Jack's ruined wedding plans. Was he still licking his wounds? she wondered, feeling empathy.

"Do you know what you want to eat?" Sue asked.

"We'll both have *Pollo Al Ajillo,*" Jack answered. "Caroline will have a cola and I'll have a beer, whatever's on tap."

Sue left after jotting their order on her pad.

Caroline looked at Jack. "Have you known Sue long?"

"We went to the same high school. She was a freshman when Eddie, Ray and I were juniors. It's been awhile since I've been here in La Casa. Sue's mother and father own the place."

"Conway?" Caroline asked, perplexed.

"Sue's mother is Spanish."

"Oh," Caroline said, and then started thinking of Jack back in high school. It made her wonder again how he'd come to live with Nina and Ray. Caroline was mulling over the etiquette of asking him when Sue returned to the table.

Sue set their salads down along with a pitcher full of the house dressing, and a basket of hot, steamy rolls. "We have a cheese dressing, if you'd rather?"

"I like this one," Caroline said, recalling the taste.

"So do I," Jack answered, though Sue obviously had remembered.

Sue smiled and left the table.

Caroline poured some dressing on her salad and passed the pitcher to Jack. He drenched his greens.

Caroline looked across the table at Jack. "Could I ask you something?"

"Sure." His eyes stayed on her.

"How did you come to live with Nina?" Caroline inquired, then qualified. "You don't have to answer if you don't want to."

"Nina and her husband took me in after my mother died. My mother was working for Nina at the time."

"I'm sorry about your mother, Jack." Caroline felt an immediate rush of sympathy.

Jack nodded.

"And your father?" Caroline toyed with her salad.

"He walked out on my mother when I was quite young. I wouldn't know him if I passed him on the street."

Caroline's compassion was all aroused. "What about relatives?"

"I guess I have some in the Midwest somewhere. My mother's family disowned her when she married." Jack brought a forkful of lettuce to his mouth, but then put it back in the bowl without having eaten any. "My mother was some lady... tough, stubborn and very loving, like Nina."

"Did she work for Nina a long time?" The devotion in his voice toward his mother and Nina impressed Caroline in a heart-stirring way. She couldn't even imagine how difficult it must have been for him, alone at fifteen.

"No, only about six months. Nina was teaching her how to cut and style hair. My mother changed jobs frequently. We moved a lot. She was always trying to better herself. The trouble was that she'd never learned any real business skills. But she was a hard worker. I think I inherited her workaholic genes."

A lull fell while they both ate their salads.

Sue, seeing that Caroline and Jack were ready, came to the table with their dinners and drinks and set everything out. "Enjoy," she said.

"Thanks," Jack replied.

Caroline still had her mind on Jack as a teen. "I'm amazed that Nina only knew you for six months when she asked you to live with her."

"Nina has a heart of gold and her husband, Raymond, was the best. They both deserved medals for not only taking me in, but dealing with me. I wasn't the nicest of kids. I had a large chip on my shoulder. I thought the world had done me wrong."

"That's understandable, Jack." The warmth of her feelings made her reach across the table and rest her hand over his.

He liked talking to her. He liked her tenderness even more, and that unnerved him. "Come on, you're not eating," he pointed out, though neither was he.

Caroline let go of his hand to spear some chicken with her fork. After she swallowed, she asked, "What happened to Raymond?" Though it hadn't come up while she'd been at Nina's, Caroline's intuition told her that he wasn't in the picture anymore.

"He died when Ray and I were eighteen."

"Oh . . . Nina hasn't had it easy."

"No, she hasn't."

"Did you and Ray get along from the start?" Caroline questioned softly.

Jack wanted to change the mood. "Are you kidding? You should know about sibling rivalry with two kids."

Caroline smiled. "Yes, I do."

"Talk about shiners. Nina and Raymond thought we were going to wind up permanently black and blue. It took Ray and I awhile to get it through our thick heads that knocking each other around was not getting us anywhere."

"I don't think you and Ray had thick heads."

Jack smiled easily. "Don't bet any money on it. The two of us can still be pigheaded."

Caroline laughed, and then they ate quietly for a few minutes.

"What do you do to get ready for your auditions?" Jack started a new conversation.

"Well . . ." She was going to make up something, then decided to be honest. "What I do is stand in front of the mirror, try to get into character, and then I sort of make faces at myself until I find one that I think works. Then I make up some dialogue. That's about it."

"Would it help any for you to try some out on me?"

Caroline slanted her head as she debated his proposal. "I guess it would depend on whether or not you'd be honest. You might be sitting here thinking I looked goofy, and then be too polite to tell me."

Jack grinned. "I thought we'd decided that neither one of us was going to be polite. Didn't I give you my word that I'd be honest with you?"

Caroline bantered. "But if you do say I look goofy, I'll be mortified. So, I don't think it will work."

"How about if we both try out some goofy looks and then we can get any self-consciousness out of the way? How's that sound?" It sounded to him like he was flirting with her.

Caroline flashed Jack her sauciest look. "We could try it. You first."

Jack looked back at her with bemusement. "Somehow I knew that I'd be first." So what was the big deal if he flirted with her a little bit? He wasn't going to let it get out of hand.

"Let's go, Corey. I'm waiting."

Jack held up his hands, palms forward to forestall her. "Give me a minute. I know there was a time when I used to be able to cross my eyes."

"That might work for goofy." Caroline put her elbow on the table and rested her chin on her hand. She teased him with a look.

Jack gave it a try, and, after a few failed attempts, he managed to cross his eyes.

Caroline giggled. "Where's a camera when you need one?"

"All right, Phelps." Jack raised his eyebrows up and down. "It's your turn."

"Umm..." Caroline flippantly arched her brow, copying his expression. "I don't think so."

Jack reached across the table and gripped her wrist, pulling her hand out from under her chin. "Don't make me get rough with you." He tried for a gangster-style accent.

Caroline made a face at him, sticking her tongue out while he held her hand to the table.

Sue came over. "Are you cruising for another bruising?" she asked Jack, aware that he and Caroline were fooling around. "What's wrong with the chicken?" She noticed neither of them had eaten much.

"The chicken is fine," Jack assured Sue.

"Yes, it is," Caroline agreed. "I guess I wasn't as hungry as I thought I was."

"Well, take your time. I'll come back."

The wonderful food had grown cold on both their plates. They'd been too involved with each other to do much eating.

"I'm finished," Caroline said. She felt foolish now trying to gobble her food down after saying she wasn't that hungry. She hoped her stomach wouldn't give her any back-talk.

Jack couldn't see himself eating alone. "You can take mine, too."

Sue started clearing the table. "How about some dessert? The flan is excellent."

"I should be getting home," Caroline said, thinking of her kids, worrying that they'd be waiting up. It was a school night.

"You can get me the check," Jack told Sue.

While Sue walked to the counter to write it up, Jack reached behind to his back pocket for his wallet.

Caroline opened her handbag and riffled around for her billfold. "I insist we go dutch."

Jack patted his two side pockets, and then he remembered where his wallet was. It was still at home on his desk.

Sue came over with the check and handed it to Jack. "It was great seeing you. Hope we'll all see more of you now," she said.

Preoccupied, Jack nodded absently.

Sue took off.

Caroline had her billfold open. "Just figure how much it is with the tip and we can split it in half. I insist."

Jack had never felt as ill at ease and disconcerted as he was feeling right then. He had never taken a woman for a meal and not paid the bill.

Caroline noticed that Jack looked distressed and was immediately concerned. "Are you okay?"

Jack shook his head. "I'm totally embarrassed." He fessed up. "I forgot that I left my wallet at home. I don't know how I could have forgotten about it. I got a ticket driving over to you this morning for not having my license. Look, sit tight for a few minutes. I'll run back to Nina. She always has money on her. I'll pay the bill, the whole bill. I do not invite women out for dinner and stick them with the tab."

"Jack, give me the check. I don't have a problem with this." Caroline tried to pull it out of his hand. He wouldn't let go.

"I have a problem with this." He'd never been in this kind of situation before.

Caroline was finding his discomfort very appealing, and it was all the more reason why she wanted to help him out. "Jack, if you don't give me the check, I'll..." She couldn't come up with a finish.

"You'll what?"

"I don't know, but you won't like it." That was the best she could come up with.

"It might be worth it to find out," he said, starting to loosen up.

Caroline gave him a cute smirk. "If I do it, we'll never be able to show our faces here again."

This time when she pulled on the check, he let her take it from his hand. "I am still embarrassed about this."

"That makes us even. I was embarrassed when you found me with my hair in tin foil this morning." She took out enough money from her billfold to include a tip and then laid it on the table with the check. Their meals were inexpensive. La Casa was not only known locally for its great food, but for its equally great prices.

Jack got up from his side of the table. Caroline got up from hers. "I owe you one," he said.

"Okay." She smiled.

They both waved to Sue on their way to the front of the restaurant. "Say hello to your mother for me and tell your father I said good-night," Jack called over, not seeing either of them around.

Out on the street, Caroline shivered. The temperature had dropped with the sun.

"Go back inside," Jack said. "I'll get the car."

"It's all right."

"Will you please let me have my way with something?"

Caroline conceded with a knock-out smile. "All right. I'll wait inside."

Caroline walked back into the restaurant. Jack ran the block. She watched for him through a window. Jack drove up in front and parked at the curb. He started out of the car to get her, but she was already coming out of the restaurant. He saw her into the car and then took his seat behind the wheel. He had the key in his hand as he looked over at her.

Their eyes met in the illumination of a streetlight overhead. Neither of them moved. Caroline had the distinct impression that he was thinking of kissing her. She felt a flutter of anticipation. Then more than a flutter. Her pulse jumped wildly.

Abruptly, Jack put the key into the ignition. He let out a breath he hadn't realized he'd been holding and began to drive. He didn't know what had just gotten into him.

Caroline was aware of her disappointment even as she was telling herself that she wasn't looking for anything to start up between them. He wasn't even her type. A businessman, a workaholic. She could just about chart his entire personality from that information alone. There wasn't any way that they were a match.

Jack turned the radio on. He couldn't think of a start for any small talk. He was annoyed with himself. A little flirting was one thing. Kissing her would have been a whole other matter. Where was his head?

Caroline was restless.

Jack was edgy.

She groped for something to say, but nothing came to mind.

He switched stations up and down the FM band, then reset the radio to AM and found a talk show.

For the entire ride back to the house, they both pretended an absorbing interest in the pedigree of cats.

Jack pulled onto the driveway. He shifted the gear into park, left the motor and headlights on. He got out of the car and came around and opened the door for her. This time she waited for him.

They stood together by the side of his car in the hazy dark.

"Good luck tomorrow," he said.

"Thanks," Caroline returned formally. "I'll let you know how I've made out." She took three backward steps.

"Okay." He didn't move.

Caroline turned and walked up the stairs and onto the porch.

Jack leaned back against the hood of his car and watched her go into the house. He was bothered by the way their evening had ended.

Chapter Five

"Mom, your hair his shorter than mine," Bobby said with a grimace. "You look like a boy."

"It will grow," Caroline assured him, but she was getting used to it and thinking of keeping it short. She was in Bobby's bedroom saying good-night. She'd already said good-night to Elizabeth. Her daughter had made only two comments about her hair, yuk and yuk. And they'd both laughed.

"Good night, Mom." Bobby snuggled in under his blanket.

Caroline bent down and kissed Bobby on his cheek. He had begun to complain about being too old to be kissed, but he let her get away with it tonight. She ruffled his hair and then started for the door.

"Mom." Bobby remembered that he had something on his mind. "Don't put any carrot sticks or celery sticks or any stick things in my lunch box tomorrow. What were those white stick things you put in on Friday?"

"Zucchini sticks. Did you like them?" Caroline asked, hopefully.

"I didn't eat them. I didn't even like how they looked. Elizabeth threw hers away, too. I saw her in the lunchroom."

"Why don't you buy lunch in the cafeteria? I like knowing you're having a hot meal. If you buy lunch, Elizabeth will, too."

"All the popular kids bring lunch in this school."

Caroline knew that was the end of this discussion. "All right. I'll just put in fruit with your sandwich tomorrow. But the two of you are going to eat all your vegetables at dinner."

Bobby wrinkled his nose, but he didn't argue. He knew his mother had a vegetable thing and there was no talking her out of it. "Make sure my sandwich is peanut butter and jelly."

Caroline smiled. "Of course." She did get their peanut butter ground fresh, and she only bought jellies that were natural and without preservatives. "See you later, alligator," she said, halfway out the door.

"Later, alligator," Bobby answered, sleepily.

Caroline left Bobby's bedroom and walked downstairs to the living room where Myra was checking the *TV Guide*. Myra had already passed judgment on her short hair and approved.

"I hate when the networks do this," Myra complained. "I can't decide which movie to watch. Tearjerker? Comedy? Or mystery-thriller?"

"You can tape one."

"I'll tape the tearjerker. I think we're out of tissues." Myra waved the guide at Caroline. "Which one do you want to see, the comedy or the mystery?"

"Oh, no. I'm not picking. The last time you did this to me, you were grouchy all night because you were sure the movie you didn't see was better than the one you saw. Anyway, I don't think I can sit through a movie. I'm going to put the kids' lunches together and make myself something to eat."

"Didn't you just come from dinner?"

"Yes." Caroline answered on her way to the kitchen.

Myra got up to follow Caroline. She still had a half hour to decide on a movie. "Were the portions small?"

"No." Caroline opened the refrigerator. "I just didn't want to eat then."

"Lousy food?"

"No. It was really good."

Myra sat down at the table. "Did he say anything about the house?"

"He's giving us some time. I just don't know exactly how long. He wouldn't let me pin him down." Caroline took out whole-wheat bread, fresh peanut butter, pure raspberry jam, and closed the refrigerator.

"It's not going to do you any good to get yourself all agitated. You'll get another part. You have talent. And if it's not this house, it will be another house. The kids will adjust if we have to go back to an apartment."

"I don't want them to have to adjust." They were already handling a divorce. "This house is perfect for us. I really feel it's going to work out." Caroline tried as ever to hold on to her optimism.

"Jack Corey seems very nice."

"I suppose." Caroline reached under the counter for environment-friendly reusable sandwich wrap.

"You don't like him?" Myra questioned.

"I didn't say that." Caroline thought about him almost kissing her, and felt goose bumps. She had to rub her arms up and down. What, Caroline asked herself with surprise, would she have felt had he followed through?

"What's the matter with you?" Very little escaped Myra's notice. "Are you getting a rash? Or hives? I knew someone once who broke out with huge hives whenever he got nervous. I may have mentioned him to you. Dennis Richardsen? We called him Denny."

"I'm sure you did mention him." Caroline didn't want to hear any Denny stories. And she didn't want to talk about Jack. "I'm not getting hives."

Caroline spread jam over peanut butter, centered each top piece of bread, sliced off crusts, and cut Elizabeth and Bobby's sandwiches into pie-shaped wedges. She sealed them with the wrap and then started making a sandwich for herself.

"He's quite nice-looking," Myra commented, studying Caroline closely.

"Who?" Caroline played stupid.

"Jack Corey."

"So what?" Caroline got defensive. "I meet dozens of nice-looking men. They're all gorgeous in show business. Looks don't mean anything. It's personality and attitude that counts."

"I didn't see anything wrong with his personality. Let me tell you something, he could have been a lot crankier after you gave him a black eye."

"It was an accident. I didn't do it on purpose." Was it her fault that something always went haywire?

Myra nodded.

Caroline thought about Jack. She couldn't seem to stop thinking about Jack. Was Myra ever going to drop the subject?

"What did the two of you talk about over dinner?" Myra wanted to know.

"This and that. As it turned out, the beautician he took me to was sort of his mother. We talked about that."

"What do you mean, sort of his mother?"

Caroline explained, and Myra thought it was a sad, but lovely story.

"I hope you thanked him for taking you there."

Caroline nodded, chewing on her peanut butter-and-jelly sandwich. But now that she thought about it, she realized she'd thanked Nina, but she hadn't thanked Jack. Of course, she could right that quick enough. She could call him up and apologize for forgetting to thank him. She could do it as soon as she stopped almost hyperventilating at the thought.

What, she asked herself, *is going on with you?*

Nothing, she answered herself. *I've just had a rough day.*

"...And you shouldn't discount every man you meet without giving them a chance." Myra stopped in the midst of her lecture. "Caroline, are you listening to me?"

Caroline blinked. "Yes, I'm listening. You were saying?"

Myra continued. "Take Jack Corey, for example. If he should call you and ask you out, you should go."

Caroline gave a short laugh. "What is there, a virus going around? Why is everyone trying to match the two of us up?"

Myra's brown eyes widened. "Who else is trying to match the two of you up?"

"Nina Sanchez." Caroline finished the rest of her sandwich. "But he's not interested, and neither am I."

But Myra was interested. "How did Mrs. Sanchez go about doing that? Did she come right out and say that you and Jack should start seeing each other?"

"She didn't come right out with it. What she did was put Jack on the spot by suggesting that he take me to dinner. Jack told me afterward what Nina had up her sleeve."

"Is that when he said he wasn't interested?"

"Yes," Caroline answered quickly, but she didn't recall him being that specific.

"Of course, then you said you weren't interested, either?"

"It didn't go quite that way, but it was mutual. Neither one of us actually spelled it out."

Myra tried a different tact. "It doesn't really matter. I'm just using him as an example. What I'm getting at is that you should be dating."

Caroline countered. "Didn't I let Stacy, my best friend since we were kids, fix me up? And not once, but twice."

Myra rebutted, "I don't call meeting someone for lunch and someone for a drink *dates*. That's not trying. Do you really call that trying?"

Caroline tried for an escape route. "Aren't you going to miss the movie?"

Myra checked the clock on the wall. "I still have ten minutes."

Caroline walked over to the refrigerator. She gathered half a dozen peaches and plopped them in front of Myra on the table. "Do me a favor. Tell me which ones are the ripest? You have a better feel for fruit than I do."

"Caroline, I just want to see you happy." Myra inhaled a peach. "You know I love you like a daughter."

"I love you, too. I am going to be happy when I know this house is ours. Please try to understand that I'm not interested in looking for, or getting involved with, a man. Honestly, I don't think there's anyone out there who would even be right for me. And it's not just me we're talking about. He'd have to be perfect for Elizabeth and Bobby."

"I am thinking about Elizabeth and Bobby, as well as you. They need a father for more than a month out of the year. Not that I ever thought he was much of a father or a husband. I haven't said anything before this, because you were trying so hard to make it work, but in all the years I've known you, I never saw the man crack a smile. All he ever thought about was making money."

"You have to be fair." Caroline wasn't going to let Myra place the entire blame on Steve. "I'm not that easy to live with."

"The man had no sense of humor." Myra ticked off one of Caroline's ex-husband's faults.

"I'm too impulsive. I always think I'm thinking things through, but I guess I don't think hard enough." Caroline listed a fault of her own. Maybe she'd even jumped too soon to try and buy the house?

"You need someone who is a little impulsive... someone with a sense of humor."

"Maybe I just need more time to get over feeling like a flop." Caroline had been brought up to believe that marriage was forever.

Myra got upset. "I don't want to hear you call yourself a flop."

Caroline gave in, but only on the surface. "All right, I won't call myself a flop."

"I don't want to see you make the same mistake that I made when my marriage failed. I was young like you and just as afraid to stick my neck out again."

"It's never too late," Caroline said fondly. "I do run into nice older gentlemen every now and then. I might just start bringing them home. Maybe for dinner?"

"There's no talking to you." Myra got up from the table. "I'm going to go watch my movie. All I was trying to say was that I think Jack is a nice person. Period." With that last remark, Myra walked out of the kitchen.

Caroline completed putting together the kids' lunches. She thought about the house, absently. She thought about her auditions tomorrow, anxiously. She thought about Jack and felt a mix of confusion and excitement.

She wondered what he was doing. How could she have neglected to thank him for taking her to Nina? She wondered if he'd gone straight home after he dropped her off?

Caroline couldn't seem to get her mind off Jack. She blamed it on Myra, and all her prompting.

Jack polished off the last of the *arroz con pollo* that Nina had brought over. He was sitting bare-chested, with a fresh pair of jeans on. He'd showered first thing when he'd gotten home.

The TV was on. He was trying to pay attention to the start of a movie mystery, but he kept getting distracted as his mind picked up on little tidbits of the day. It had been one helluva day! He smiled to himself, thinking of Caroline with her hair all wild and the way she'd told him "what for" in her bathroom. He pictured her in La Casa making a face at him. He imagined her standing in front of a mirror making faces at herself.

Gingerly, Jack touched the swelling around his right eye. He knew he should call the real estate office in the morning and list the house again to quickly cover his bases. It was the smart thing to do. But he knew he'd feel like a heel if he didn't give her a little time. He thought about the dinner he owed her. He started getting a good head of steam going on that thought until he brought himself up short. Was it possible that he was becoming his own worst enemy?

Caroline practiced in front of her mirror for less than a half-hour. She just couldn't make herself concentrate. She was still thinking of calling Jack, because she really had to thank him. She even walked over to the phone in her bedroom three times, but she didn't lift the receiver. She wasn't sure that she fully accepted her motivation at face value. There was a niggling notion rattling around in her head that calling him on the premise of thanking him might just be an excuse.

Caroline made a face at herself in the mirror. This time, she wasn't acting.

Jack went to his phone. He dialed Caroline's number, but he hung up before completing the call.

What are you doing, Corey? Chasing her?

I owe her a dinner. I'm just getting it out of the way. Setting it up.

Do you have to do it right now? Think about it a while.

Jack thought about it. He didn't have to be a genius to figure out that he was a little attracted to her. Not that he couldn't ignore it. But why go out of his way to ignore it? He already had enough to do. He was busy nursing his shattered ego. He was even busier overhauling his bruised heart.

He was very busy.

Caroline joined Myra in the living room three-quarters of the way through the mystery-thriller. Myra was seated on the couch, fast asleep. Caroline watched the movie through to its conclusion, knowing Myra would want to know who had wound up being the killer. Of course, the man who looked like the one who did do it, had done it. Sometimes Caroline wondered if casting directors had eyes. That reminded her that if she didn't get a good night's sleep, she was not going to look alive tomorrow.

Caroline woke up Myra, filled her in on the end of the movie, and then both women walked upstairs to their respective bedrooms.

Caroline showered, brushed her teeth and creamed her face. She put on her buttercup-yellow cotton pajamas. She checked her alarm clock. It was nearly eleven-thirty. She set it to ring at 6:00 a.m. She didn't have to be at Marty Gold's office until noon, but she always got up with her kids.

Caroline looked at the phone on her nightstand. No, she was not going to call Jack now. It was too late.

Jack opened the couch and made up his bed. He was really beat. He hadn't slept well the night before in New Jersey. Feeling thirsty with Nina's *arroz con pollo* kicking in, he walked over to the refrigerator and fetched what was left of a quart of milk. He brought the vee of the container to his mouth, and slugged down the last few gulps. The TV was still on, just making noise. He was physically exhausted, but still edgy.

Caroline had the small-screen TV on in her bedroom. She turned the volume all the way down, and then she grabbed her handbag. Finding her book of phone numbers, she quickly flipped to *C*. Without giving herself any more time to rethink the idea, she sat down at the side of her bed, picked up the phone and dialed Jack's apartment. If he wasn't home, he wasn't home. If he was asleep, she'd apologize for calling so late and hang up quick. She was not going to be able to relax until she thanked him.

Jack picked up his phone on the first ring. "Hello."

"Hi. It's Caroline." She was nervously twisting the phone cord around her finger. "Did I wake you?"

"No." He was dumbstruck that she'd called. "Actually, I was thinking about you. Hold on a second. I just want to turn off the TV." He nearly fell over one of his sneakers in his sprint to do so. He was back on the line in less than a second. "Hi," he said quickly.

"Hi." Caroline thought her voice sounded a little froggy. She turned her head from the phone to try and clear her throat.

From his end, Jack listened to what sounded like she had a case of hiccups. "Are you all right?"

"Yes," Caroline answered tersely, self-conscious that he'd heard her. But she had heard something, too. "Did you say you were thinking about me?"

He would have preferred not having given her that information. He wouldn't have, if she hadn't caught him off guard. "I was just wondering if you were practicing for your auditions tomorrow."

"Oh . . . I did, but I'm finished now."

"I see."

She could see herself doing a scene with him from *When Harry Met Sally.* She'd say, "I'd like us to be friends." He'd say "I don't think men and women can just be friends."

"Caroline?" He wondered if she'd hung up on him.

"Yes." She was now coiling the phone cord around her free wrist and was forced to bend closer to her nightstand with each turn. "I called because I realized that I never thanked you for taking me to Nina. I wanted to thank you."

"You paid for dinner," he reminded her, smiling. "I call that thanks." It was the perfect opening for him to invite her for a return treat, but he didn't. He decided to wait. He'd wait until they closed on the house, which wouldn't be long if she got one of the parts she was sure she was going to get tomorrow. Then they could celebrate. He'd take her someplace fancy. And she'd go her way. And he'd go his.

"Well... anyway." Caroline battled to extricate her wrist from the phone cord.

He knew she was getting ready to end the call. He didn't want to let her go. "How are you getting into the city tomorrow? Are you driving? Or taking the train?" He tried to keep her talking.

"The train." Caroline shook her wrist to get her circulation back now that she'd gotten her hand out from the phone cord. "I know your yard is right next to the station. I could stop by when I come back and let you know how I made out."

Jack considered that possibility. He liked the idea, which was why he backed off. "I don't think I'll be at the yard much. I have a number of jobs scheduled," he lied. He did have a job to do in the morning. But Monday afternoons, he and Ray stayed at the yard to catch up on billings and paperwork. "It would be easier if you just called."

Caroline got his message loud and clear. And she didn't have to think long to get it. He was giving her a brush-off.

Caroline gritted her teeth. Did he think she was making a play for him? Was she? No way, she reassured herself. "Fine. I'll just call. I've got to go now. Good night."

Jack just about wedged in his good-night before the line went dead. "Well, fine," he said and slammed down the phone, feeling annoyed.

Caroline turned the volume back up on her TV. She got into bed with the remote control.

Jack turned his TV off. He set his alarm clock, banged the light, yanked off his jeans, and got into bed. He was asleep before his head even hit the pillow.

He was in a church, and he was walking down the aisle. He was pretty sure he was getting married. There were a couple of clues. One, he was wearing a tuxedo. Two, there was a jazz trio singing "Here Comes The Groom." He called out, "Hey, isn't the bride supposed to be walking down the aisle? I think we've made a mistake here."

Somebody laughed. Then there were a lot of people laughing. The trio had to raise their volume to be heard.

He kept on walking. It was a very long aisle, and he was moving in slow motion. He had to strain, but he could see that there was a bride waiting for him at the altar. She was dressed in gads of white. He didn't think he'd be able to see her face even if she was turned toward him. Her head was covered with a long veil. Still, he was fairly certain that he knew who the bride was. Who else could it be?

He reached her finally. And she turned with her hand out. No, both hands out. And her hands were full of papers. He knew they were bills. "The house needs to be painted again." She didn't sound very happy.

He took the bills from her and stuffed them in his pockets—his jacket pockets, his pants' pockets, his back pockets. With his hands finally free, he lifted the front of her veil. But it wasn't Jill! It was Caroline! And her hair was all striped again and sticking out.

The reverend asked, "Well, do you?"

He tried to speak, but he couldn't. His tongue was stuck to the roof of his mouth, and the roof of his mouth tasted like peanut butter.

The reverend was getting impatient. "Well, what is it with you? You want her, but you don't want to pay?"

There was a drum roll. He looked at Caroline looking at him. She was smiling one of her million-dollar smiles. "I may have forgotten to tell you that the kids have to go to the orthodontist. Give me money."

He wanted to give her the money for the kids. He stuck his hands in his pockets and all the bills fell out. He was digging deeper and deeper when he decided that what he needed to do first was pull her into his arms.

He got her in his arms, wrapped her close, and they kissed and turned, and kissed and turned, and somehow or another his foot caught on the hem of her train, and then they were falling and rolling, and rolling and falling. She whacked him one, right in the eye. Only now she was Jill and she was saying, "I don't think I love you anymore. . . ."

Jack woke in a cold sweat. He looked at his watch. The luminous dial told him he'd only been asleep for twenty minutes or so. He felt as if he'd been dreaming for hours. Only that wasn't a dream. It was a nightmare.

He got out of bed and turned his TV back on. What he needed was to focus on a different mind-set.

Caroline turned her TV off. No more fooling around, she told herself. She needed to get to sleep. She adjusted her blanket. She tried a number of different positions and finally settled on her back. She closed her eyes and began to create a fantasy in her mind to get herself comfy.

She got dressed in her white linen suit.

She reconsidered.

Was the white suit right? She did have her pink dress and her black suit to wear tomorrow.

No, white was right.

Caroline smiled at her rhyme and then moved her fantasy right up to the auditions.

She pictured herself reading for both roles. She pictured herself being offered both parts. In fact, since this was her fantasy, she decided there would be another director from another studio down the hall who would just happen by and hear her read, and he'd come over and offer her a role in his soap.

She had to pick the one she wanted, and each director was begging her to pick his show. Begging, begging, begging...

Caroline fell asleep....

Pots and pans were banging as she walked into the kitchen. She'd had a long day on the set, but she had new energy now that she was home. Elizabeth and Bobby were sitting at the table, engrossed in their homework, munching on carrot sticks. They looked up to wave test papers at her. Of course, they'd both gotten *A*s.

Myra was standing at the stove slamming pots around, cooking.

Caroline was baffled. "I thought we'd agreed that I'd do the cooking, because you hate cooking."

Myra answered, "I'm only cooking because *he's* home, and *he's* hungry. You know *he* doesn't like your cooking. Remember, you make things that are just too romantic."

Caroline nodded, remembering the time she set the curtains on fire because she wanted him to eat by candlelight. Only, she couldn't remember who *he* was. "Who is *he?*"

Myra shrugged. Bobby called out, "Elizabeth and I want to know if *he* is staying?"

Caroline tried to puzzle it out. She just wasn't sure. "I think I'll go ask."

She walked to the living room, but she couldn't get in. There was a bulldozer parked in the center, taking up most of the space.

What, she wondered, had happened to her furniture?

She got up on her toes to try and see into the cab of the bulldozer. But she still wasn't tall enough. She was just about to go back to the kitchen for a step stool when *he* stuck his head out the window.

"I hope you don't mind, hon," Jack called to her. "I had to bring some work home tonight. Work, work, work..."

"Oh, no," Caroline mumbled, thrashing around in her sleep.

Chapter Six

"Hi, Marty," Caroline said sprightly as she stepped into Marty Gold's office.

Marty Gold didn't answer. His lips parted, but nothing came out. He sat behind his desk, peering at her through his wire-rimmed glasses. He took his glasses off and peered at her again. He wiped his glasses with the show hankie from the front of his dark gray suit jacket. He put his glasses back on and waved her to a seat in front of his desk. He set his handkerchief back in place.

Caroline sat down. She crossed her legs demurely and lowered her white shoulder bag to the carpeted floor. Caroline knew a bad sign when she saw one. The way Marty was looking at her was not a good sign. She shouldn't have worn her white suit, which was an imitation of a Chanel cut. Her pink dress would have better advertised her curves. How many times had Marty spoken to her about packaging?

"Different," Marty spoke, his fingers tapping his close-shaven face.

Caroline swallowed hard. Marty Gold only worked on his face when he was perturbed. It was her hair. That was it! It was her hair.

"I could get a wig," Caroline suggested quickly, jumping to rectify, yet, another one of her mistakes.

Marty pushed his leather swivel chair back from his desk and got up to walk. He tapped his face, one side after the other.

Oh, no, Caroline thought, tensely. Walking and tapping... Walking and tapping had to be worse than tapping alone. Was he going to say that he didn't want to handle her anymore?

Marty came to an abrupt halt. He was in his late fifties, short, not quite five foot eight, slim, natty and manicured. Caroline had been with him three years now, and she was still thrilled that he'd taken her on. He was smart, determined, full of dynamic energy, though a bit quirky. If one listened to the theatrical grapevine, and she did, then no agent worked longer or harder for his clients than Marty Gold. Rumor had it that no other agent was more ingenious at cooking up a deal and then haggling the best terms.

"I'm not sending you to those auditions," Marty said decisively. His hand came up, this time to smooth his still-dense, sliver-gray hair.

Caroline's stomach was on an elevator ride to her throat. She was starting to have difficulty breathing. This was awful.

Marty perched on the corner of his desk, facing a rejected Caroline. He pressed his intercom.

"Yes, Mr. Gold," came Cheryl Lynn's cheery voice.

"Call Allison Raye. Give her the information on the two auditions I set up for Caroline Phelps. Tell her I just got a ring on them and that I want her to read." Marty knew he didn't have to detail diplomacy to Cheryl Lynn. She'd been his secretary for ten years now. She read his mind better than he did.

Caroline waited for the ax to fall. She prayed that at the very least, Marty wouldn't say, Don't call me. I'll call you.

Then, just as Caroline was considering the possibility that she would never breathe normally again, Marty smiled.

"You look mah-vel-ous." Marty imitated Billy Crystal doing his Fernando bit from "Saturday Night Live." The routine had been out of fashion for a long time, but Marty still liked to use it.

"What?" Caroline was in shock. Was she hearing right?

"Hmm," Marty said, working on his face.

"Hmm?" Caroline questioned tremulously.

"Those auditions weren't right for you. Not the 'new' you." Marty was thinking out loud.

"I'm still the old me. I could be the old me with a wig." Caroline blew a breath. "Wait a second—I have it. I get a wig from the make-up department at the studio there before I read. What do you think?"

"Hmm," Marty answered.

"Hmm?" Caroline echoed, toying nervously with her emerald-green beaded necklace that had looked so right with her white linen suit when she'd gotten dressed that morning.

"Give me a profile," Marty said quite suddenly.

Caroline was so startled she yanked on her necklace. The beads came apart.

"Profile," Marty repeated bearishly, uninvolved with her beads.

Snapping to attention, Caroline turned to give Marty her left profile and then her right profile. Her eyes were on her beads on the floor. As soon as she thought she'd given Marty enough of a look, Caroline got down on her hands and knees to pick up rounds of emerald glass from the kelly-green carpeting.

"Give me your right profile again," Marty bellowed.

Caroline did a little bunny-hop on her knees to accommodate Marty as she continued her search. Finding what she hoped were all of her beads, Caroline stood, hands full, and then sat down again. She dropped the beads in her lap, turning her knees inward to make a pocket in her slim skirt. She opened her white leather purse. She dumped the beads in her bag. She could just see someone coming into Marty's office, tripping on one of her beads and suing her.

"You'll get new pictures taken," Marty started off slowly, then went into rapid fire. "Make an appointment for next week . . . or as soon as you can. I have an idea for you. It's brilliant, even if I have to say so myself. Do you have something a little showy, a little sexy, to wear. If not, you'll buy something. Not black. Not red. Not to the neck. Not too low. We want to advertise, not broadcast. You'll bring a date. Not someone in the business. It's black-tie. He'll need a tux. If you need money to buy something for yourself, I'll lay it out." Marty paused to think again.

"Marty?" Caroline asked, her voice squeaky, her head spinning. "What are you talking about?"

"I'm talking about the party that NBC is throwing this Saturday night. I've been invited to parade all my newest faces, as has every other agent in town. You, my little sweetie, have got yourself a new face. We're going to go and see what we can get ourselves with it. *Capice?*"

"I think so." But just to be sure, Caroline reiterated. "You want me to go to a party Saturday night with a date. You want me to wear something a little sexy, but not too showy. Not black, not..."

"Not red," Marty filled in when Caroline stumbled over the other color he'd tabooed.

"Right, not red. And we go and see what we can get."

"Exactly." Marty smiled.

Caroline was pleased that she'd gotten all the details correct, but where did that leave her? It left her without a job.

Marty was on the intercom. "Cheryl Lynn, you'll give Caroline two invitations for the NBC thing on Saturday."

"Right, Mr. Gold," Cheryl Lynn repeated. "I already took two out for her after I called Allison."

Marty grinned at Caroline as he raised his finger from the intercom. "That dyed redhead out there scares me sometimes. I think she knows when I have to go to the bathroom before I do."

Caroline smiled, but it was forced. She couldn't get beyond the fact that she didn't have a job. And wouldn't even have the prospect of a job until after Saturday. What was she going to tell Jack?

Marty stood.

Caroline got up from her seat, knowing she was being dismissed.

Marty Gold put his arm around Caroline's shoulders as he saw her to the door. "Are you still liking it out in the sticks?"

"It's not the sticks. It's only forty-five minutes by railroad to New York. And I love it," Caroline answered, then said, "Isn't there anything else you can send me on this week?"

"Trust me, Caroline. Saturday's the ticket." Making an about-face, Marty left Caroline in the outer office with Cheryl Lynn.

Cheryl Lynn held out the two invitations that she'd placed in a small manila envelope.

Caroline was feeling practically numb as she accepted the envelope.

"I like what you did to yourself," Cheryl Lynn said. "He likes it, too." She nudged her head toward Marty's closed office door.

"Thanks, Cheryl Lynn." Caroline heard her voice, but it sounded as though she was standing in a fog.

Cheryl Lynn apparently could see Caroline was upset. "Marty knows what he's doing. You can trust him."

"I do," Caroline said, trying to get a grip on herself. She did trust Marty Gold's judgment. When Marty Gold said he had a brilliant idea, he had a brilliant idea.

"How are the kids?" Cheryl Lynn asked. She took a personal interest in most of Marty Gold's clients. There were a few she didn't like. She never gave a moment of her time to the ones with airs and affectations. She liked Caroline Phelps.

"Great." Caroline smiled a genuine smile. "How are your kids?"

"Terrific. My oldest is up in Rochester. He's finally decided to go for his master's degree. My middle guy just graduated from Albany. He'll be going to law school next year. And my daughter is at college in Plattsburg. She's a sophomore already. It's so quiet in the house, my husband and I are going crazy."

Caroline commiserated. "I can't even think of Bobby and Elizabeth going off to college."

"They're gone before you know it." Cheryl Lynn sighed. "Did Marty tell you what not to wear for Saturday and to bring a date?"

"Yes." Caroline nodded.

"Do you know who you're bringing?"

"I haven't the foggiest notion." Caroline added that dilemma to her list. Then she thought of Jack, which was really a riot. What could she say to him? I don't have a job yet. I can't buy the house yet. I have a feeling that you'd prefer to avoid me, but would you mind putting all that aside and escorting me to this party that I have to go to on Saturday night?

The intercom buzzed. "Well, take care," Cheryl Lynn said, before responding to Marty's ring.

"You, too," Caroline replied, and left The Marty Gold Theatrical Agency.

The sidewalk was packed with pedestrians; businessmen with briefcases, women with labeled shopping bags. Messenger boys pedaled on bikes in the midst of taxis and trucks. Horns blasted impatiently. Caroline opened her white leather shoulder bag, dug through her green beads and pulled out a copy of the Long Island Railroad schedule. She checked her watch. It was ten to one. There was a train leaving Penn Station at one-fifteen. If she got a cab, she might just make it. The next train out at three-forty would bring her into the beginning frenzy of the rush-hour crowd. And she wasn't up to any additional frenzy.

Sticking two fingers in her mouth, Caroline stepped off the curb between two parked cars and began to whistle. This city girl knew how to get herself a cab.

Caroline was at Penn Station with six minutes to spare. What happened next happened so fast, Caroline didn't have the chance to react until after it happened. She was in the main lobby, just getting set to walk out the doors to Track 8 with her train ticket in her hand. The next thing Caroline knew she was sitting on the ground and a young guy was running off with her handbag. She saw him only from the back. He had longish brown hair, and he wore a white T-shirt and cutoff jeans. And then he was gone and her train was being announced.

Caroline heard a man shout over, "Are you all right?" But nobody came to check.

Shaken, but not hurt, Caroline found the manila envelope with her Saturday night invitations on the marble floor. She picked it up. She drew herself up to her feet. As she did, one of the heels snapped off her white leather pumps. She did the only sensible thing she could think to do. She limped out to Track 8 and climbed onto the train. Fortunately, her ticket was still in her hand.

"You know what your problem is?" Ray asked.

"I've got a few," Jack responded. "Which one are you referring to?"

The two men were in the trailer at the yard, sitting behind their respective desks with ten feet of assorted clutter between them.

"You're still smarting over Jillian. That's your biggest problem," Ray said, making a paper airplane from one of their statement forms.

"I'm not still smarting. But I hope I've gotten smarter." Jack re-added the statement he was working on.

Ray tossed his paper airplane at Jack. It changed flight mid-course and landed on a beat-up, brown leather couch to one side.

Jack put his pen down and looked directly at Ray. "If you have something on your mind, why don't you just give it to me straight?"

"You want it straight? All right. I'll give it to you straight. I think you're going after the Taylor deal because you feel there's more prestige in belonging to a big name, but I don't think your heart is in it. I remember how you used to talk about building this business up, just the two of us. And I don't hear that excitement when you talk about Taylor."

Jack was silent. He thought about Ray's remark. Well, maybe he didn't feel that old excitement. But so what? "What's wrong with a little prestige?"

"Nothing. If that's what you want, and it's not just a reaction to Jill stomping on your ego." On the last word, Ray drew italic signs in the air with his fingers.

"Don't take this show on the road," Jack said curtly. "The Taylor deal is going to be right for us. I know it is. Just cross those fingers of yours that Caroline gets a part today."

"Speaking of Caroline, Mom told me that the two of you went out last night. How'd it go?"

Jack crumpled the statement he'd been writing on and tossed it in the garbage can under his desk. "We went to La Casa for a bite to eat. We didn't go 'out.'"

"Are you going to ask her out again?"

Jack was getting way out of joint. "Didn't I just say that we didn't go out in the first place?"

Ray smiled easily. "That's what you said. So, are you going out with her again?"

Jack threw his pen down. "No, I am not going out with her again. I don't intend to see her until we close on the house. Satisfied?"

Ray shrugged. "You planning to become a monk?"

"No. I'm just not looking for an involvement."

"What's wrong with an involvement? Wasn't that you who just a few months ago wanted to settle down and do the family thing?"

"That was then. This is now."

"Personally, I think you're attracted to her."

"Well, if I am, I'm going to keep a lid on it."

"Why's that?" Ray asked, doodling on a statement pad.

"I think she's as materialistic as Jill."

Ray gave his brother an I-don't-believe-it look. "What'd she say to give you that idea?"

"Nothing. I'm just listening to my instincts."

Ray chuckled. "Instincts? Instincts, my eye. You're just plain scared to jump back into the water."

"Do me a favor and keep your opinion to yourself...."

"Gloria liked her, too, and Gloria's got good instincts."

"You and Gloria can join her fan club. Now can we get back to work?"

"Yeah." Ray looked down at his desk in disgust. He'd bet they'd be doing mostly paperwork when they hooked in with Taylor. And Jack didn't like paperwork any more than he did.

Caroline got off the train at the Rocky Hill platform. Actually, she hobbled off, walking unbalanced.

She looked around. Her car wasn't far away. Only it was locked and her keys were in the handbag that had been stolen. Caroline felt the pockets of her suit jacket, hoping for some loose change to call home so that Myra could drive over with the extra set of car keys. She didn't have any loose change.

Caroline debated. She couldn't see herself going up to a stranger to ask for some change. She could try to find a policeman. Or she could stand blubbering. That wouldn't have been hard to do.

She could see Jack's yard from where she stood. She could even see Jack's car parked in the yard. She was thinking that he could be out with one of his bulldozers, but Ray might be around.

Caroline was not up to seeing Jack. She needed time to muster her courage before telling him her latest bad news. Only she did need a phone.

Mentally crossing her fingers that Jack would be out but that Ray would be in, Caroline wobbled down the platform stairs. She needed to hold tight to the handrail to keep from falling.

Jack and Ray both looked up as the door to the trailer opened. Jack was the first to speak. "Caroline?" His eyes widened. She looked, to him, like she'd been shot out of a cannon.

"I'm sorry to bother you." As her fate would have it, Caroline wondered how she could have expected anything else but to find him here. "Could I please use your phone?" She stood lopsided, disheveled, her white suit streaked with dirt, but she had her chin up.

Jack was out of his seat. "What happened to you?" He was very alarmed.

"I was mugged." Caroline said it valiantly, trying not to make it into a big deal. But it wasn't easy to do when she was fighting back a sudden rush of tears.

Jack enfolded her into his arms. He held her gently, but firm. "Are you hurt?" His voice was jerky.

Caroline shook her head, feeling newly upended in reaction to being close to him. "I got pushed, and I fell down when he took my pocketbook. But I'm not hurt."

"He pushed you!" Jack got so upset he could have punched walls.

"Jack, maybe she should sit down," Ray suggested, standing next to the two of them.

Caroline had nothing against that idea . . . she needed a little space. She was trying to keep her composure, but it was impossible with Jack so near and comforting.

Jack could have whacked himself for not having thought of that first. "Come on, Caroline." He put his hand to her arm to draw her forward. "Let's sit on the couch."

Caroline swayed like a drunken sailor as she started to walk. Jack looked down at her feet and ascertained the cause of her difficulty. He switched his hand from her arm and swung it around her waist. Tucking her against his side, he brought her over to the couch.

Caroline sat down, her breathing shallow. Jack and Ray sandwiched her in between them. Jack took her hand in his.

"Are you sure you're not hurt?" Jack asked again, scrutinizing her face for any sign of distress.

"I always meant to take lessons in self-defense," Caroline muttered helplessly. "I just never made the time." She looked down at her knees and blurted the worst of it out, her frustration at the surface. "And I didn't get a part. I didn't even get the chance to read."

"You'll get other chances," Jack said soothingly.

Caroline kept her head down. "Don't sound like you're not annoyed that I didn't get a part. I know you are."

Jack leaned forward, placed his free hand to her chin and lifted her face. "I'm not annoyed. Stop trying to read me. You're not very good at it."

Caroline didn't see any annoyance when she looked into Jack's blue eyes. She saw warmth and sensitivity, and she felt his blatantly masculine magnetism working on her again. She had to look away to regain the slim hold she had on her equilibrium.

Ray was not having any difficulty reading Jack. He glanced at the way Jack was holding Caroline's hand and the look on his face. Whether Jack wanted to admit it to himself or not, he was smitten with her.

Jack caught the wisenheimer expression Ray sent his way. Uncomfortable with Ray's obvious evaluation, Jack broke eye contact, but he didn't let go of Caroline's hand.

"Did this happen when you first got into the city?" Ray asked, turning to Caroline.

"No." Caroline shook her head. "After...after Marty said I wasn't right for the parts. He's put me on ice for a week . . . a whole week. And I have to go to this party Saturday night."

"What kind of party?" Ray asked before Jack got the words out.

"A network thing," Caroline mumbled. "I have to find someone to take me. Someone not in the business. Someone who won't mind renting a tux. And I have to wear something showy, but not red and not black." She was rattling.

"Jack could take you," Ray said. "Jack has a tux. Right, Jack?"

"Right," Jack answered, thinking about how long it had been since the two of them had slammed each other around.

Caroline turned crimson. Sure, she'd thought of asking him, but she wouldn't have. And she certainly hadn't wanted Ray to put him on the spot.

Jack got to his feet. He took Caroline's hands and helped her to stand. He was relieved to see some color in her face. "Come on. I'm taking you home."

Ray called out. "Hey, Jack, why don't you take the rest of the day? Stay with Caroline. I've got things under control here."

Jack turned his head and smiled. "Good. Then you can finish up the billings on my desk." With that, Jack carefully assisted Caroline out of the trailer with a strong supporting arm curled around her waist.

Neither Caroline nor Jack spoke on the ride to the house. Caroline, for her part, was worn too thin to talk, but she did notice that his shiner looked a little better.

Jack was occupied worrying about her. She looked so woebegone. He wanted to do something to cheer her up.

Jack parked his car on the drive. He got out and helped Caroline out on her side. He walked her up the stairs of the porch and to the front door.

"I'll be back in an hour," he said, having a brainstorm. "Put on sneakers and something comfortable that you can move in. When I get back, we're going to the beach."

Caroline blinked, then stared at him. Had he said the beach? "There's not enough sun to go to the beach."

"We're not going for the sun. We're going so that I can give you a few lessons in self-defense."

She eyed him quizzically. "Why would you want to go out of your way for me?" He was right. She did have trouble reading him.

"I don't want you running around not knowing how to protect yourself. Are you up to a little exercise?"

Caroline's face lit up. Jack's concern gave her an incredible jolt of vivaciousness. "I'm up to some exercise." Only, who was going to protect her from him and the heady feelings she didn't want him to evoke?

"I'll be back in an hour," Jack said and then left.

Jack was back at the house exactly an hour later. He was still dressed in faded jeans and a navy-blue polo. Caroline opened the door before he rang the bell. She wore Nike sneakers, khaki shorts and a man-sized white cotton shirt, sleeves rolled, tails hanging out. Jack couldn't stop himself from checking out her legs. She had dynamite legs.

"Let's jog to the beach." He thought it would be good for her to limber up. "I'll go slowly."

"I'm a pretty fast runner." She saw herself dazzling him.

Jack grinned. "I take challenges seriously. I'm not going to give you any quarter just because you're a woman. Are you sure you want to challenge me?"

Caroline gave Jack a big smile. "I'm sure."

"Okay. You're on." He was glad to see that she was behaving more like her spunky self. "On the count of three. One... two... three."

Caroline sprinted. Jack kept close. He didn't have to really stretch to do so. Then Caroline really sprinted, running hard. And Jack had to pump it. They were both winded by the time they hit the deserted neighborhood section of beach two blocks away.

"Tie," Caroline said, panting.

"Whooo..." Jack sucked in the pungent air from Long Island Sound. "Where'd you learn to run like that?"

"I ran track in high school and the two years that I went to college. I've stayed in practice. You're pretty good yourself. It's nice having someone to run with."

Jack smiled. "I had expected to come off a lot better."

Caroline raised impudent eyes. "I'm sorry about that."

"I bet you are." Jack lunged and tackled Caroline down to the sand.

Caroline looked up at him in shock as he pinned her hands up over her head.

"This is your first lesson in self-defense. Stay on your toes," Jack teased.

"Not fair. You didn't give me any warning." Caroline tried to sound light, but her heart hammered so disturbingly it was difficult for her to even speak.

Jack winked. "Sweetheart, bad guys don't give out warnings."

"Oh, I get it. You've been scamming me all along." Her gaze made a circle and came back to him.

Jack thought she might have him sized up at this moment. He'd extemporized when he'd brought her down to the ground. But now he was up to no good.

Don't, he warned himself, don't even think of it!

Rolling to the balls of his feet, he pulled her up with him. He brushed sand from his hair. She brushed sand out of hers. And their eyes met. Both felt the electricity.

"Well . . ." Caroline said inanely, her pulse jumping.

"Well," Jack repeated, edgy and antsy. "Shall we continue?"

"Are we going to be on the sand again?" Caroline was all jittery.

Jack shook his head. "No, no more sand." He took a few backward steps. He took a few deep breaths. He took a few more backward steps. "Okay, now. Come toward me, and when you get to me raise your hand."

"Okay." Tense, Caroline started toward him, raising her hand.

Jack took a hold of her wrist when she reached him. Taking care not to exert any pressure that might hurt her, he brought her to her knees. Then he helped her up. He felt her tremble.

"You're not nervous, are you?" He studied her.

"Me? Nervous? Of course not," Caroline lied, her heart beating much too rapidly.

Jack backhanded a thin film of sweat on his brow that had nothing at all to do with exertion. "Now you try."

Caroline grabbed his hand as soon as he raised it and tried to copy his move, but didn't get it. Her concentration was way off center.

"Try again." Jack fought off the idea of showing her some exercises that had nothing at all to do with self-defense.

Caroline took his hand again. This time she got it. Jack made her repeat the maneuver one more time, battling with himself to keep his mind on the right course.

"That was great." Caroline smiled, excited by her accomplishment.

Jack enjoyed watching her. "Are you ready for more?"

"Ready." Caroline did some bouncing in place, all exhilarated.

"Stay where you are." Jack walked about ten feet away, getting his protective instincts back in place. "I'm going to turn around, and I want you to come up behind me. When you get directly behind me, I want you to try and get a stranglehold around my neck."

Caroline stopped her bouncing to shift nervously from foot to foot. "Are you going to flip me over?"

Jack gave her a snappy look. "No, but I'm going to show you how it's done. I promise that I won't let you fall."

"Where did you learn all this?"

"I took two years of judo lessons when I was in my teens. Ray's father figured it would help me work out some of my hostility."

"Are you still hostile?"

Jack grinned. "Come on at me and find out." He turned his back to her and waited, knowing she would.

Caroline approached him, her sneakers quiet on the sand. Jack didn't need to hear her to know when she was near. He was already familiar with her scent. She smelled like early spring, lilac in bloom. Even her shampoo had a lilac fragrance. He was certainly acquainted with her shampoo.

Caroline brought her arm up around Jack's neck. She had to stand on her tiptoes to do so. That was the easy part. The hard part was the jangling of her nerves at her body contact with him. This was all getting to be a little too much for her.

Jack thought he had his cool back, but he didn't. Equally jangled, he went through the motions fast; grabbing her arm, bending forward, lifting her off the ground, and then putting her back on her feet.

Standing in front of him now, Caroline stammered. "Well, I think that's it. What do you say? Is that it?"

"Maybe you should just give it one try." But he was just as reluctant as she was.

Caroline gulped air. "All right, but just once." She turned her back to him. Jack put his arm around her neck. Caroline gave a yank to his forearm and bent to the side. Jack felt her losing ground. He knew she was going over and he tumbled forward trying to cushion her fall.

Jack twisted his shoulder as he landed on the more firmly packed sand closer to the water's edge. Caroline landed right on top of him.

Jack groaned as he tried to move.

"Are you hurt?" Caroline asked anxiously, squirming off of him.

Jack spoke through his teeth. "It's my shoulder. I pulled it out a little."

"I can't believe all I've done to you. I've given you a black eye, and now I've made you twist your shoulder." She was very upset. "I'm a jinx. I really am a jinx."

Jack wasn't going to let her feel bad. He cupped the back of her head to keep her looking down at him. "I told you that there was a hex on me. What makes you think it was your jinx and not my hex?"

"Take my word for it. I'm unlucky."

Jack inserted his fingers into the collar of her shirt. "I don't think so," he whispered and didn't feel any pain at all in his shoulder as his other hand found its way to the small of her back.

Caroline knew they were talking about something, but she'd forgotten what it was. All she was aware of was her mouth inching closer to his while his fingers did delightfully exciting things to the back of her neck.

And then the tide came in.

Ice-cold water washed over them from their sneakers to their knees.

Caroline jumped up.

Jack flipped to his feet. "I think I'm going to start carrying a change of clothing in my car."

"That's an idea." Caroline gave Jack a thumbs-up sign. "And maybe I should walk around with a first-aid kit."

Jack smiled and Caroline smiled back.

Working the sprain in his shoulder, Jack bent down to roll up his jeans. "So what time do you want me to pick you up on Saturday?"

Caroline's eyes narrowed. "You don't have to take me." She didn't want him to take her if he was feeling roped in by Ray.

"You know another guy with a tux that you'd rather have take you? Think before you answer. I don't take rejection well."

"Can't say that I do." Caroline's eyes brightened. Maybe he didn't feel roped in...

"Good answer," Jack said playfully.

Chapter Seven

Jack rechecked his black bow tie in the rearview mirror before getting out of his car. He was parked in front of Caroline's house. It was Saturday night. Four days had gone by since he'd seen or spoken to her. He'd thought of calling her a hundred and one times. He'd even come up with a number of excuses that might have sounded legit, but he'd resisted. He'd made up his mind to resist. He could resist a little chemistry if he wanted to resist it.

Taking the porch steps in a quick gait, Jack got to the front door and rang the bell. He caught his reflection in the curtain-covered side panel. He was wearing the tuxedo he'd bought to be married in. He'd expected to feel twangs and pangs putting it on, but he hadn't.

Jack rang the doorbell again. Obviously, no one had heard his first ring. Caroline would be nervous, of course. She had her hopes pinned on tonight. He envisioned himself being her support—her towering strength. He envisioned himself being her hero. But did he have the panache to mix with her crowd?

Suddenly uptight, Jack looked straight ahead as the door finally opened. He expected it to be Caroline, but it was her son who stood at the threshold.

"I'm Bobby." The child opened the door wider for Jack to enter. "My mother isn't ready yet. She said we should keep you company."

"Okay." Jack smiled. He saw Caroline's daughter then. She'd been standing just behind her brother.

Bobby made a face at his sister. "This is Elizabeth."

Elizabeth had herself all decked out. Her long nutty-brown curls were piled up on her head and held precariously with an assortment of clips. She had on green eye shadow, pink lipstick, a yellow blouse that had to be her mother's, judging from the fit, white tights, a green plaid skirt and a pair of her mother's high heels.

Jack thought she looked adorable, pretending to be all grown up. The distraction helped to ease his tension.

"We're supposed to go in the living room," Elizabeth said, being the hostess.

"Elizabeth, you look ridiculous," Bobby jeered, adding an aside for Jack. "She thinks she looks like Madonna."

"I don't look ridiculous, Bobby." Elizabeth sashayed around. "You don't know how girls are supposed to look. And I do look like Madonna, 'cause her hair is dark sometimes."

Running her hand along the wall for balance, Elizabeth made her way to the living room taking little mincing steps as she struggled to walk in high heels that, to begin with, were three sizes too large for her feet.

Bobby mimicked his sister's walk behind her back, showing off for Jack as they followed Elizabeth into the spacious living room.

Jack sat down on a nubby mauve couch and took in the personal touches of Caroline's eclectic personality: he appreciated the blend of colored enamel furniture, comfortable upholstery and smattering of Victorian frill. There was a white console TV at one end and lots of houseplants.

Jack suddenly realized that the kids were staring him down. "Where's Myra?" he asked, making conversation.

"She's helping my mother with her dress," Bobby answered from a stain-guarded rose armchair where he'd plopped. "You know how girls can't always make up their minds."

Jack suppressed a grin at Bobby's man-to-man exchange.

"Girls can make up their minds the same as boys," Elizabeth rejoined from the other rose armchair. Swinging out her leg, Elizabeth accidentally kicked off one of her shoes. She quickly retrieved it and then sat at the edge of the chair with her feet touching the floor to keep the high heels on.

"Everyone has trouble making up their mind sometimes." Jack tried some diplomacy.

"Do you know about steps?" Elizabeth was on to a new subject.

Jack looked at her quizzically. "I don't know what you mean."

"Like if my mother gets married," Elizabeth explained. "Then we'd have a step. My father got married."

"Elizabeth, you have such a big mouth," Bobby sneered. "And your lipstick is dumb!"

"I am not dumb," Elizabeth stormed. "And I can talk if I want to." She stuck her tongue out at Bobby.

Not to be undone, Bobby pulled out a floral throw pillow from behind his back and threw it at her.

Catching it, Elizabeth was just about to throw it back when Jack intervened. "I don't think your mother wants the two of you fighting."

After a few second's debate, while she estimated the adult's authority, Elizabeth handed Bobby the pillow and smiled at Jack with feminine sweetness.

Boy, do they learn young, Jack thought with amusement. "Now, what about steps?"

"I don't like steps because they're mean," Elizabeth answered bluntly.

"Has your father's new wife been mean to you?" Jack figured that she'd have to be cold as ice not to warm to these two. Granted, they could be a handful, but that was the way kids were supposed to be.

"We haven't seen her yet. We don't even see our father, but we will see him in..." Elizabeth paused. "In maybe a year. He lives in California now."

"Elizabeth, we're going to see him in July when we have the summer off from school. That's not a year."

"If it's after school, then it's a year," Elizabeth insisted.

"I'm sure that the lady your father married won't be mean," Jack inserted, sensitive to Elizabeth's worry. He'd bet Bobby was just as concerned. Poor kids... Jack hoped they weren't feeling rejected. He wondered how Caroline was reacting to her ex-husband getting remarried.

"Everyone says that steps are mean." Elizabeth repeated what some kids at school had told her.

"I have a step," Jack offered. "I have a stepmother and a stepbrother, and I had a stepfather, but he died."

"Did you cry when your stepfather died?" Elizabeth questioned, wide-eyed.

"Yes, I did." Jack was aware of Bobby listening to him as closely as Elizabeth was.

"Is your stepmother mean?" Elizabeth asked.

Jack shook his head. "She's great, and she's always been wonderful to me. It's pretty special to have an extra family. You get to have more people to love you and to do things with you."

"My father didn't like doing things with us." Bobby faked indifference.

"That's 'cause he was very busy." Elizabeth spoke on her father's behalf. "Bobby, don't still feel bad that he couldn't go to your Father and Son Picnic."

"Who said I ever cared about that?" Bobby denied still being hurt. "And you shouldn't still feel bad that he couldn't get to your play."

Jack, his heart turning over, looked from Elizabeth to Bobby and marveled at the way they could be fighting one minute and in the next minute tend to each other's disappointments.

"I'll tell you what I think," Jack said, putting his two cents in. "I bet when you see your father in July he'll have a lot more time to spend with the two of you. And you'll do lots of great things together because he will have planned for it."

"That's what Mommy said," Elizabeth affirmed.

"Elizabeth," Myra yelled from the top of the stairs. "Do you know where your mother's navy blue high heels are?"

Elizabeth looked up at the ceiling with her big brown eyes and then down at the navy blue heels on her feet.

"You're in trouble," Bobby said, shaking his head. "Give them to me. I'll tell Myra I found them in the kitchen."

Elizabeth had a better idea. She took the navy heels off, then innocently tried to push them under the couch.

Tickled by her antics, Jack pulled them back out. "Don't worry." He gave Elizabeth a reassuring smile. "Let me handle it."

Taking Caroline's shoes, Jack walked out of the living room and met up with Myra at the bottom of the stairs.

Myra saw the heels in Jack's hands. "Let me guess. Elizabeth?"

"Elizabeth." Jack grinned.

"Why don't you take them on up?" Myra suggested deviously, obviously setting up an opportunity for Caroline and Jack to see each other alone. "She's decent."

"You don't think she'll mind?" Jack hesitated. He didn't want to wait to see her any longer, but he was edgy and jumpy again.

"She won't mind," Myra responded, going down the stairs and leaving Jack with no other choice. Myra didn't see any reason why she shouldn't join in on the matchmaking that was already going around.

Caroline was bent over, looking under the bed for her shoes, when Jack got to the door of her bedroom. Jack nearly gasped as he took in Caroline's unintentionally provocative pose. The silky material of her navy-blue dress with white polka dots was hiked up practically to her hips, spotlighting her gorgeous legs and sexy derriere. Bracing himself against the doorjamb, Jack sought some of the towering strength he'd planned on providing for her. He completely lost track of the cute remark he was going to make about Elizabeth.

Caroline stood, turned, and was brought up short as she saw Jack at her door. Stunned, she stood with her mouth open. She hadn't expected to see him in her bedroom. She hadn't imagined how lethally handsome he'd look in a tux.

They both spoke at once.

"Oh, hi..." Discombobulated, Caroline couldn't come up with much of a sentence.

"Hi," Jack returned, feeling like he'd stutter if he said more, not that he'd ever stuttered before in his life.

Shakily, Caroline smoothed the skirt of her dress, fiddled with the straps that rested off her shoulders. And stared at him. "Your shiner is better." Her pulse was speeding. "Is your shoulder okay?"

"Uh-huh." Jack dropped his gaze long enough to take in her beautiful creamy shoulders and impossibly small waist. "I have your shoes."

"My shoes?" Caroline looked down at her nylon-clad feet and then up to spot her shoes in his hand.

Standing glued to the doorjamb, Jack reached out his arm to hand them to her. The cerebral decision he'd been making the last four days to resist her chemistry was being blown, quite quickly, to tiny little bits. Mind over matter wasn't helping him any.

Caroline was just as unsettled by Jack's particular brand of sexuality. She came up just near enough so that she could stretch out her hand to accept her shoes without getting too close. But she was all thumbs and dropped them as soon as she had them in her hands.

Caroline and Jack both bent at the same time and knocked heads. Jack grabbed the shoes with one hand and rubbed his forehead with the other. "Are you okay?" he asked.

"Yes." Caroline rubbed her temple. "I'm sorry. That was my fault."

"No, it was mine." He smiled at her and wondered what the chances were that he'd still be in one piece by the end of the night.

Caroline took the shoes from Jack's hand. She went over and sat down at the side of her bed and put them on. Why did these things happen to her? She'd had a whole fantasy going about making a ravishing impression on him.

Fascinated, Jack watched her. He caught a small frown on her face after dragging his eyes all the way up from her toes. "What's the matter?"

Caroline's face colored. "Nothing. I just wanted to make an entrance."

"Oh..." Jack's eyes flashed over her again. "You have." He gave her a low wolf whistle.

With her blush deepening, Caroline whistled right back at him. "You have, too." She was amazed to find herself drawing a flush from him for a change.

Jack was zapped. He'd handled his share of compliments, and he had ample experience with flirtations. But he was zapped. That brash smile she'd used and the way her mouth had puckered to whistle had zapped him.

Caroline, disconcerted by her own outrageous manner, swung around to her bureau to compose herself. She tried cooling her cheeks with the backs of her hands. This constant blushing was really unlike her. Caroline was fairly certain that she remembered herself being somewhat sophisticated before he'd stepped into her life.

"I just have to find my lipstick and we can go." She turned back to him, but didn't meet his eyes.

Jack didn't need much prompting to single in on her mouth. "I think I can help you with that." He took a step, planning to head downstairs to ask Elizabeth if she'd seen her mother's lipstick. But that wasn't the direction his feet took him. Before giving himself a chance to weigh the pros and cons, Jack moved toward Caroline. If he was going to be zapped, he decided on the way, he wasn't going to be zapped all alone.

"Jack?" Caroline's breath caught with anticipation. She'd only suspected until now that she was attracted to him. Now she was sure... Too sure!

Jack gave a second's thought to the possibility that someone might walk in on them. He didn't want to place her in an awkward situation.

He kissed her lightly, holding himself back with tremendous difficulty.

"Yes?" he asked.

"Oh." Caroline lifted her eyes up to him. "What was that for?"

Jack improvised. "That was for good luck. We do want to ward off all those hexes, don't we?" He drew a soft line across her temple with the tip of his finger.

"Yes." It was absurd, Caroline decided, to go weak in the knees over such a slight kiss. But she had to steady herself with a hand to her bureau just the same.

Jack worked on restraint. "I'll send Elizabeth up." In another moment he was going to stop reasoning. "I have a feeling she knows where your lipstick is."

Jack took himself out the door and beyond temptation. Caroline took some long breaths, aware that the spicy essence of his after-shave mingled with the sweet scent of her Chanel No. 5. She wanted him to come back, kiss her for real, put a claim in. She hadn't bought his bit about warding off her jinx and his hex. She hadn't bought it for a single moment. He was attracted to her. And she knew it.

Stepping away from her bureau, Caroline took some more full breaths. She was wondering if his heart had been thumping the way her heart had been thumping, as Elizabeth walked in with her lipstick.

Ten minutes later, Caroline and Jack were in the car driving to the NBC bash. Jack turned the radio on.

"Is there any particular music you'd like to hear?" he asked.

"Anything as long as it's not hard rock or heavy metal. My nerves are already frayed." Caroline put out a hand to show him she was shaky.

Jack found a station playing soft rock and roll. Hoping to ease her tension, he started singing along, thinking his off-key voice might give her a laugh.

"Bad, huh?" he asked after a moment or so.

Caroline smiled. "Not as bad as mine."

"Prove it." He perused her with a grin.

"You don't really want me to do this? You don't know what you're asking for."

"If I'm willing to hang myself out to dry, you'd better be prepared to meet me halfway."

"Well, if you put it like that..."

Caroline sang along with the Eurhythmics while Jack kept his head cocked. She could carry a tune if she wanted to, but she played along with him and made sure her voice cracked.

"Well?" Smiling, Caroline sought Jack's eyes.

Jack affected a sober, judgmental expression as he flashed her a look. "I think it's too close to call."

Caroline laughed. "You take that back, or I'll make you sorry. Anyway, I sound great in the shower."

Jack gave her an open leer. "I can't just take your word for it. You're going to have to prove it to me."

"In your dreams," Caroline quipped.

Jack grinned, satisfied that he'd gotten her to relax. Now, if he could only do something about his edginess . . .

"I know what we should do," Caroline said. "Sing together. That way, we could drown each other out."

Jack managed only a peek at her this time. The traffic had gotten heavier. "Maybe together we'll only be half as bad."

"Whose half are you speaking about?" Caroline teasingly slugged Jack in the arm.

"Am I in physical danger here?"

"You better believe it."

"Then my half, of course. But just you wait until I get my hands free of this wheel."

The festivities were well under way when Caroline and Jack arrived. The network had requisitioned one of their larger studios for the event. The room was set up with chairs and tables covered with white linen cloths. There was an elaborate buffet that promised a treat for the most discriminating taste. But it was the long bar that drew the crowd, while a combo of musicians played lively rock and roll on a small stage.

"Do you think we should go up with the band?" Jack joked, helping Caroline slip out of her midnight-blue suede jacket.

"I think we've gotten too good for them." Caroline spotted Marty and waved.

Marty was seated at a table with his wife, Louise. He was sampling from the plate he'd filled. He'd been keeping an eye out for Caroline. She was the last of his clients to arrive.

Jack checked Caroline's jacket at the counter set up near the door. As Caroline took a step forward, Jack stopped her.

"Now, you show them who's boss." He shot her a smile of encouragement.

"Got it," Caroline bantered. "And I'm going to get you your business deal," she added with determination.

She just about bowled him over at this point, because somehow or another, he'd forgotten about his vested interest in her success. Covering up quickly, he smiled. "I don't doubt that for a moment."

Caroline led Jack over to Marty's table. Marty and Louise got to their feet as they approached.

"You look better than mah-vel-ous," Marty said, in exactly the same way he'd said it to all his guests, male and female. Marty prided himself on being impartial. Still, he did have a special feeling for Caroline. He admired the way she'd handled the knocks she'd taken in the last year.

"Thanks, Marty," Caroline answered and kissed Louise's cheek. She'd met Louise Gold only once before, but Louise was the kind of woman who made one feel like an immediate friend.

Jack and Marty were amiably shaking hands and exchanging names before Caroline had the chance to do the honors. Caroline did introduce Louise. The older woman looked polished and elegant in a soft beige wool dress with a simple cameo on a gold chain around her neck.

"It's a pleasure to meet you, Jack," Louise said, smiling.

"It's my pleasure," Jack said charmingly.

Marty spoke to Caroline. "There are plenty of mucky-mucks here. They've sent executive producers, directors, writers. The whole shebang. They're all wearing white carnations so you can distinguish them. Meet as many as you can. The scuttlebutt is that they are planning to add two entirely new soaps to their daytime schedule. Smile, eat something, drink something, stay calm. And did I say smile?"

Caroline smiled. "You said smile."

"Okay, then go mingle." Marty shooed her away.

Caroline and Jack took off.

"How about some wine?" Jack asked, needing a drink himself.

"White." Caroline nodded. "I'll probably spill it. At least white won't show too badly."

Jack grinned. "No talk about jinxes tonight."

"Okay," Caroline conceded, trying to get herself to relax.

They circumvented the dance floor, which was starting to fill with couples intent on strutting their stuff. Jack elbowed space for them at the bar and then ordered two white wines. He didn't intend to drink much or drink anything strong. He was driving.

Three hours later, Caroline and Jack sat down for a respite with Marty and Louise. There were other people at the table now, some of Marty's clients and a couple of other agents who'd come over to chat.

Marty whispered to Caroline. "How are you holding up?"

"About as well as a melon in a supermarket," Caroline whispered back. "But I did get my name jotted at least eight times. I hope my health insurance will cover the surgery I'm going to need to remove the smile from my face."

Under the table, Jack squeezed Caroline's hands. He could hear her conversation with Marty.

"You see Kathleen Fox Emery at the end of the buffet table?" Marty questioned, directing Caroline's attention with a quick eye signal.

"Yes." Caroline looked over that way. Kathleen Fox Emery was another of Marty's clients. Caroline had met Kathleen a number of times. She recalled Marty comparing Kathleen to a young Susan St. James. Kathleen, with her long dark hair, soft features and slim figure, did have a look that crossed stunning with perky.

"She's talking to Ron Gallagher," Marty continued on. "He's vice president in charge of daytime programming. He's one you want to meet. If you get his attention, hang in."

"Gotcha," Caroline responded, then force-fed herself some shrimp.

Jack still had some food left on his plate when Caroline pushed back her seat. He got up with her. He had managed to eat a lot more than she had.

"Thanks," Caroline murmured to Jack as they headed for Gallagher.

"For what?"

"For being here. For staying at my side." She was enticed by the way he handled himself.

Jack winked, enjoying the smile that touched her mouth, knowing this one was real and just for him.

A couple of others had joined Kathleen Fox Emery in Gallagher's circle by the time Caroline and Jack arrived.

Kathleen had the floor. "I just can't imagine that there's going to be a strong audience for imported soaps."

A voluptuous platinum-blonde chimed in. "The Australians are so hard to understand unless they speak English." She spoke with a lisp.

Jack exchanged a wide glance with Caroline, and she sent him a quick grin. There'd been moments all night when Jack thought he and Caroline were surrounded by weirdos. The platinum blonde was probably as nutty as they came.

The only male actor in the group, a young good-looking guy with pitch-black hair and gray eyes, responded to the blonde. "They do spcak English in Australia."

"I don't call limey, English," the blonde lisped, twisting deliberately in her low-cut black gown to give Gallagher an eyeful of her cleavage.

Kathleen gave Caroline a surreptitious poke, knowing that Caroline was trying to stifle a laugh. Caroline noted that Kathleen looked sensational. Her umber-brown strapless sheath dramatized her copper-colored eyes, and her thick hair was brushed loose, appearing tousled and sexy.

"Well, we're just going to watch the ratings for a while before we get on the bandwagon," Ron Gallagher stated, taking in the two newcomers with one sweep before his gaze rested on Caroline.

Caroline manufactured her freeze-framed smile as Ron gave her a once-over.

For the first time this evening, Jack was not at all thrilled with the look Caroline was receiving. Jack took stock of Ron Gallagher. With envy, Jack checked out bronze skin, good build, symmetrical features, light brown eyes, a full head of dark brown hair, and a tuxedo that hadn't come off of any rack. Jack estimated he was in his late thirties, early forties.

"Who's your agent?" Ron asked Caroline, taking out his small notepad from the breast pocket of his jacket.

"Marty Gold." Caroline watched him write. "Caroline Phelps," she added when he seemed ready.

Ron put his hand out to Caroline after putting his pad away. "It's real nice to meet you, Caroline," he said, all suave.

"Same here." Caroline shook hands with him. Jack thought Gallagher held on to her hand longer than was necessary.

Caroline turned to Jack with a fixed smile on her face. "Mr. Gallagher, I'd like you to meet Jack Corey."

Jack was feeling aggressive as Ron extended a hand his way. As they shook, each tried their best to exert the most pressure. Even though Jack knew he'd won out, he still chided himself for starting the activity. But something about Gallagher rubbed Jack the wrong way.

"So, Caroline, what do you think of the current craze to import soaps?" Gallagher ogled Caroline's chest.

"It will put some of our best people out of business." Caroline was so excited by Gallagher's regard that she missed the direction his critique had taken.

But Jack didn't miss it. The hairs on the back of Jack's neck stood on end. Combative, Jack possessively strung his arm around Caroline's shoulders, trying to block some of Gallagher's panorama.

"Creativity always seems to take second place to dollars and cents," Ron returned with a cool, savvy smile that he shifted toward Jack.

Oh, yeah! Jack was thinking. He could be just as hip as Gallagher any day of the week. He only lacked the guy's bucks, position, prestige and maybe a couple of inches. But what really had Jack hot under the collar was the way Caroline was standing there totally enraptured, listening to Gallagher talk.

Jack squeezed Caroline's shoulders. "Let's dance." They hadn't yet tonight, and this seemed a perfect time.

Caroline blinked a couple of times as she looked at Jack. Didn't Jack understand? Talking with someone like Gallagher was what this was all about. Why was he trying to pull her away?

In the background, the musicians had switched to an energetic Latin rhythm.

"Maybe later." Caroline gave her attention back to Gallagher.

"I'd like to dance," Kathleen volunteered, standing at Jack's other side.

"Great," Jack responded, making a split-second decision. If he couldn't drag Caroline away, he was not going to stand and watch her with Gallagher.

Caroline felt dismayed as Jack dropped his arm from around her and walked off with Kathleen. Out of the corner of her eye, Caroline continued to watch Jack and Kathleen even as she tried to partially focus on Gallagher.

"Can you mambo?" Kathleen asked Jack as he drew her into a dance position.

"Yes." Jack let the music imbue his spirits. He angled a look over to Caroline and observed, with satisfaction, that he had her attention now.

Kathleen and Jack danced like they'd practiced together for years. There was so much excitement and sensuality in their performance that everyone else on the dance floor stood to the side to watch their movements.

Caroline, completely disregarding Gallagher, had her eyes pinned on Kathleen and Jack. A couple of times, Caroline spotted Jack's mouth move next to Kathleen's ear. Caroline had no doubt that he was trying to make time with Kathleen. That rotten so and so...

"That guy is hot," Gallagher commented, giving Jack a professional eye. "Is he with Marty Gold?"

"He's not in the business," Caroline answered tightly. *Monkey business is more his style.*

"Well, if he decides he's interested, tell him to give me a call," Ron said.

Caroline couldn't believe this was happening. Jack had kissed her for good luck, but he was the one getting lucky—and she wasn't thinking about Gallagher's proposal as she gauged that point.

Chapter Eight

Jack and Kathleen danced to a full set of Latin music. Jack was ready to call it quits when the group changed to a new rhythm, but Kathleen, with a high-voltage smile, insisted they take a turn at the reggae beat. Not wanting to be impolite, Jack conceded. For some reason that escaped him, Jack couldn't seem to give the alluring Kathleen his total absorption. He would have expected to be fascinated by her. She was beautiful. She had a great smile. She had a terrific body. The vibrations were there, and he wasn't in a stupor. Jack wished he knew what his problem was....

Jack shifted a glance at Caroline just in time to catch her bending nearer to Gallagher. Ron Gallagher, not one to let an opportunity go by, placed a hand casually on Caroline's bare shoulder—her beautiful bare shoulder. Jack scrutinized Caroline's face, and she still appeared to be utterly in awe over whatever Gallagher was saying. Jack couldn't understand how Caroline didn't see that

Gallagher was sleazy. Jack wondered if Caroline had a naive trust in people, or was it her natural optimism that caused her to place herself in dubious situations without a thought to the outcome. Didn't it occur to her that Gallagher might be construing all those smiles of hers as a come-on?

Jack had no trouble at all figuring out where Gallagher was coming from. Gallagher, plain and simple, was using his status to come on to her.

Caroline smiled up attentively at Ron Gallagher every time she was aware that she had Jack's notice. She wanted to convey to Jack that she didn't have the slightest interest in what he was doing on the dance floor with Kathleen. But in the process of keeping track of Jack, Caroline missed most of Ron Gallagher's conversation. For all she knew, she was making a fool of herself, smiling at all the wrong pauses.

Then again, Caroline didn't have to work up much effort to see herself as a fool. She had to have been a fool to think that Jack was singularly attracted to her—singularly being the operative word. She wouldn't have been surprised if he was attracted to every female in the room. At least the ones under forty.

"Do you and Caroline have something serious going?" Kathleen asked now that she was dancing close enough to Jack to commandeer his ear.

"Serious?" Jack seriously wanted to wring Caroline's neck. "I wouldn't say that we had something serious going."

"Just friends?" Kathleen used a seductive tone.

"Ah..." Jack hesitated. He didn't know quite how to label his relationship with Caroline. They had a business situation going, but there was more to it than that. Only he couldn't seem to come up with a category that fit.

Kathleen got tired of waiting for Jack to answer. "Have you known each other for long?"

"Not long." Jack thought back to the day he'd helped her get the tin foil out of her hair. She'd been so vulnerable as she'd looked to him for reassurance. Who would have helped her out if he hadn't been there to bolster her spirits?

A smile cornered Jack's mouth as he mused about the shiner he'd gotten for his effort.

"Does Marty handle you?" Kathleen was asking.

Jack shook his head. "I'm not an actor."

"What do you do?"

"I have a small excavating, grading and landscaping business." Jack was about to mention that he was on the verge of a big business deal, but he wasn't looking to impress Kathleen.

Kathleen put a hand to Jack's forearms and felt his muscles. "I didn't think this was a build purchased from a gym." Kathleen puckered her bottom lip provocatively.

But Jack was too distracted to critique Kathleen. He was busy observing Caroline again.

"I seem to be monopolizing this conversation," Ron Gallagher said. "Now, you tell me more about you."

At the interval, Caroline sent Ron a half smile. Peripherally, her concentration was glued on Jack and Kathleen. The two were dancing close enough now to where she stood with Ron that Caroline could almost reach out and touch them. Or stick her foot out in his way... Stop it, Caroline scolded herself.

"Are you going to make me check up on you?" Ron Gallagher's eyes moved over Caroline with pure male interest. "Or are you going to volunteer something for me to go on?"

Jack looked at Caroline. In the nick of time, Caroline turned her head to smile up at Ron. She saw the expectant expression on Ron's face and figured she was due to respond. "I'm sorry," she said. "The music is so loud I didn't hear you."

"I asked you to tell me a little something about yourself." Ron tipped his head closer and breathed in her perfume.

Caroline said the first thing that came into her head. "I suppose I should mention that I'm a bit of a fraud." Caroline tempered the remark she hadn't meant to make with what she hoped was a fetching expression.

"That sounds intriguing." Ron grinned. "And just how are you a fraud?"

"I'm not a new face. I was on 'Days to Remember' for close to four months. They only recently worked me out of the script. Marty Gold decided that since I've changed my look that I qualify as a new face."

"I think you have a great face, but I'll take a look at some of your work on Days and let you know which face I think works best. Give me your home phone number and I'll give you a call." Ron took out his pen and black leather pad from the inside pocket of his tuxedo jacket.

Caroline was taken aback by Ron Gallagher's request. Since when did a producer call an actress instead of her agent? But then, having a casual connection with Ron Gallagher might just make a pivotal change in her career. Caroline couldn't pass it up even with her common sense making a nuisance of itself.

People were starting to call it a night. "I guess it's getting to be that time." Kathleen raised her eyes to Jack as the group finished playing.

Jack did not miss the opportunity spelled out in Kathleen's look. "Who did you come with?"

"Gregg Truit. He's one of Marty's clients. Gregg's the dark haired guy that was standing with me when we were all talking with Gallagher. We're friends . . . just friends." Kathleen checked to see if that information drew any spark on Jack's face.

It didn't.

"I'll help you go look for him," Jack offered, being courteous, but anxious to get over to Caroline and save her from herself.

"That's all right. I'm sure I'll find him at Marty's table tallying up the take for the night. Thanks for dancing with me. You're great."

"You're great, yourself." Jack exchanged smile for smile and compliment for compliment.

Kathleen took off for Marty's table. Jack went to collect Caroline. Caroline was laughing with Gallagher as Jack approached. But Caroline hadn't even been listening to Gallagher's joke close enough to catch the punch line. She was just showing amusement to be courteous. And she was glad that Jack had walked up at that juncture. Caroline laughed even heartier, wanting Jack to think she was having an amazingly good time. It was too much of a laugh to suit Jack.

Forced to cool his heels and feeling something akin to intense frustration, Jack waited impatiently for Caroline to lose the humor. He dug his hands into the pockets of his tuxedo trousers and thought about taking Gallagher out back and rearranging the egotistical smirk on his face. When Caroline finally did deem to give him a glance, Jack drew her aside with a firm hand to her waist.

"Everyone seems to be leaving. Are you ready to go?" he asked crisply.

Caroline stuck her chin up in the air and pulled free of Jack's hold. "Yes, but I could get a ride with someone else if you'd rather make other plans." Why had she said that? She didn't have the vaguest idea how she'd get home.

Jack's expression turned volatile. How had Gallagher gotten so far with her so fast? There was only one answer. Those smiles she'd been giving him had been a come-on...

"I brought you and I'm taking you home," Jack retorted in a low, gritty tone. If she thought he was going to let her leave with Gallagher, she had another guess coming. The guy was a lech.... "Is there anyone left here that you feel you need to talk to?"

Caroline didn't bother to check out the room. Instead, she peered closer at Jack. Where did he come off bullying her around? "There isn't anyone else that I need to talk to," she answered, rankled.

"Fine then let's say our good-nights." Jack could hear himself sounding barely civil. But it was a step up from the way he was feeling.

Caroline hardly had a chance to say good-night to Gallagher before Jack had grabbed her arm and moved her alongside him over to Marty's table.

An annoyed Caroline and a thorny Jack both said good-night to Marty and Louise and Kathleen. They were the only three at the table.

Marty aimed a kiss somewhere in the direction of Caroline's left cheek. "I'll call you as soon as I hear something."

Caroline showed Marty that she had her fingers crossed. She didn't bother to tell Marty that she had given out her home phone number to Gallagher. Besides, Jack was already hustling her off to the coat-check counter. Caroline had to use a longer step to keep up with Jack's loping stride.

Jack tried to assist Caroline with her jacket, but Caroline yanked it out of his hands and put it on by herself. She was really ticked off by his dictatorial conduct. Jack muttered in exasperation under his breath. Caroline saw his mouth move, but she couldn't see what he had to be irked about. She was the one with a reason to be riled.

Outside the building, Caroline and Jack walked to the car without saying a word. Jack's hand shot out to swing open the passenger door before Caroline could get to it herself. Jack was not playing any contests with her tonight.

Caroline got in with her head held at a haughty angle. Jack closed her door and walked around to climb in behind the wheel. He ran a hand over his face and through his hair. Caroline was pointedly aware that he wasn't looking at or speaking to her. Well, she didn't want to look at him or speak to him, either. Still, the silence was a killer. The race of the motor was almost a welcome noise as Jack turned the key.

Caroline fumed. She was doubly steamed because she couldn't fathom any excuse for him to be angry. She had offered to free him up for the balance of the evening so that he could go on making time with Kathleen. Caroline was positive that was what Jack really wanted to do. She mumbled under her breath, but Jack didn't see her mouth move.

Jack drove the Manhattan streets, heading for the Long Island Expressway. He was holding the wheel so tight his arms were tense from the effort. His jaw was clamped so hard that his teeth hurt. None of this was like him. Why was he getting himself so keyed-up over a woman he wasn't planning to pursue?

Caroline sat rigidly staring out her side window. She was as near to the passenger door as she could get, but she was still too close to him as far as she was concerned. The area within the two-seater Toyota was uncomfortably confining. Caroline checked to make sure the lock on her door was in place. The way Jack was whipping around each turn, she might very well fall out. And he'd probably drive blocks before he even noticed, and even then, he'd no doubt only notice if he caught a whiff of air from the open door.

After a long, intense silence, Jack turned the radio on, and then off, then on, and off, and on again. He didn't care if he broke his very expensive stereo system.

Caroline reached for it and turned it off. She didn't want to hear any music reminding her of the way he'd danced with Kathleen.

Spitefully, Jack turned it back on.

Sullenly, Caroline turned it back off.

Jack seared her with a look that seemed to say he'd like to throw a hex on her.

Caroline was not intimidated in the least. She was too angry to be intimidated.

"Fine, no music," Jack flared.

"You are acting like such a juvenile," Caroline said, giving an exemplary performance of acting composed. She didn't want him to know how upset she felt. He was sure to chalk her temperament up to jealousy.

More than her words, the tone she was using was driving Jack crazy. "You're the one acting like a juvenile." Jack's voice was tense.

Caroline lost the slim hold she had on her control. "I..." She jabbed herself, but then had to squelch the start of a tirade as Jack stopped to pay the toll at the entrance to the Queens Midtown Tunnel.

"What were you going to say?" Jack prompted her after driving away from the toll booth.

Caroline looked directly at him. Jack squared a look directly back at her. And the electricity of suppressed anger and emotion crackled back and forth between them. Caroline didn't answer immediately. She was busy counting to ten in an attempt to find some poise.

Jack had no patience left. "Don't start something with me that you're not planning to finish," he informed her, pulling his bow tie open and letting it dangle around his neck. Jack released the rhinestone studs from his starched collar with irritation curling the corners of his mouth. To think he'd even worn this damn monkey suit for her...

Caroline finally responded to Jack through gnashed teeth. "My point is that I was willing to let you make other plans." But she hadn't wanted him to make other plans. She hadn't wanted him to dance with Kathleen. She hadn't wanted him to notice Kathleen. And she didn't want him to know now that she was suffering the pangs of rejection.

Jack stiffened. "Aren't you magnanimous..."

Once more, Caroline counted silently to ten. "I wasn't being magnanimous. What I was doing was trying to let you out of an obligation so that you could go your own way."

Jack zinged her with a glance. "Oh, I know exactly what you were doing. You wanted me out of the way so you could leave with that jerk."

For seconds Caroline sat openmouthed. When she spoke, her voice was incredulous. "What jerk?"

"Gallagher." Jack didn't bother to closet his sarcasm. "Did you think I wasn't aware of the moves he was making on you all night? The only thing I haven't figured out is why I should care if you want to be an idiot and go along with him."

Caroline couldn't believe Jack's gall. "How dare you call me an idiot? For your information, Gallagher was not making moves on me. We were talking business. You were the one with the moves."

Jack stared at her in astonishment. "I wasn't making any moves."

Caroline's eyes flashed. "What do you call what you were doing with Kathleen?"

"Dancing," Jack countered heatedly, looking back at the road. "And I would have rather been dancing with you."

"Do you expect me to believe that?"

Jack rolled his head toward her again. "I asked you, didn't I? And what's more, I've already told you that I'll always be honest with you."

Caroline conceded—but not out loud—that Jack's first remark was true. He had asked her to dance. And since she was starting to feel better, Caroline didn't want to debate the latter even with herself.

After a few moments of silence, Jack said, "Caroline, I didn't mean it when I called you an idiot. If you'd like to, you can call me a name or two to make us even."

Suddenly Caroline's anger dissolved completely. "I couldn't have danced with you, anyway. I don't know how to dance to Latin music."

Jack's mouth tilted to an intimate smile. "That's not a problem. I'll teach you."

"When?" Caroline blurted.

"Right now," Jack answered impulsively as he spotted a rest area off the side of the highway.

"What are you doing?" Caroline looked around, startled, as Jack drove onto the rest area and parked the car. There were no other cars around. Not at this hour. There was hardly any traffic on the expressway.

"You'll see." Jack was going through his collection of cassette tapes. He quickly found the one he wanted, slipped it into his tape deck, and left the car idling in park.

"Are you crazy?" Caroline's heart beat faster with vivacity.

"Probably." Jack winked over at her. He turned the volume on high. He powered the windows down. And after working her lock and his lock open, he got out of the car.

"We can't dance here," Caroline protested as Jack opened her door.

Jack hunkered down. "Why not?" There was a temptingly masculine grin on his face.

"I don't know." Caroline resisted, but it was the opposite to what she really wanted to do. She was more than anxious to put herself in his arms.

Jack tugged her. "I'll lift you out if you don't come willingly."

Caroline was willing. Was she ever willing... But she did make a show of putting up a little fight before she got out to stand in front of him.

"So what do we do?" Caroline smiled while the moon ascended further into the heavens. The gleam of the car's headlights shimmered around them against a night sky bathed with a twinkling of stars. Caroline thought she might be wacky, but she couldn't imagine a more romantic setting.

Jack arched a brow. "Before I show you any dance steps, you have to answer a question for me."

"What's the question?" Caroline slanted her head, examining Jack with his tuxedo rumpled some, his shirt opened at the neck, his hair less groomed. How could she deny that she was attracted to him?

Jack took Caroline's hand. His eyes stayed fastened on her. A slight breeze lifted her hair, creating a golden halo around her face. "Did you want Gallagher to take you home?"

"He didn't even ask me." Caroline's eyes were bright. Was it possible that Jack had been jealous of Gallagher all the while she'd been jealous of Kathleen? It was possible, Caroline decided with heart-stopping elation.

Jack wasn't satisfied yet. "What if he had asked you?"

"I would have said no." Caroline wondered how Jack could possibly think that she would have wanted to leave with Gallagher. Wasn't it obvious to Jack that she had wanted him to be the one who wanted to take her home?

Jack was mollified, but he wasn't quite finished with his interrogation. "Who were you going to get a ride with, then?"

Caroline looked down at her toes. "I was stumped by that myself. But I guess I would have asked Marty to see if he could get me a taxi or a limo. Or I would have taken a room in the city overnight and caught a train in the morning."

A big smile spread over Jack's face, and he squeezed Caroline's hand. He felt the best he had all night, but he was still puzzled. "Why did you try to shove me off?"

Caroline squinted at him. "Before I answer you, you have to answer a question for me first."

"All right. Fair is fair. What's the question?" Jack was beginning to recognize that narrowed look of hers as part of the demeanor she presented whenever she wasn't sure of herself. He wanted to tell her that she could always feel confident with him.

"Did you want to take Kathleen home?" What if he had, and Kathleen had shot him down? No, Caroline reconsidered, Kathleen wouldn't have shot him down.

"Absolutely not. Not even for a second." Jack was being totally straightforward with her. "Caroline, in case you don't know, Kathleen doesn't hold a candle to you."

Actually, Caroline thought that Kathleen held a blowtorch to her, only she decided not to point it out. Instead, Caroline gave Jack her very best smile. "Are you going to show me how to dance to this music?"

And then Jack did what he'd been wanting to do all night. He stopped trying to fake himself out and drew Caroline into an embrace.

They stood motionless to the beat of the music, listening to each other's breath, and their own pulses racing in their ears; smelling each other—the trace of her cologne, the remnants of his after-shave—and the cool air, orange-flavored shrimp, and a dash of exhaust fumes.

Caroline trembled. "What dance are we going to do?" She spoke in an attempt to cover her self-consciousness. Her body shivered from head to toe.

Jack could have come up with many things he wanted to do with her. Dancing didn't even make the list. "The cha-cha. Okay?" Jack took an irregular breath while he tried to get his mind in sync. But only because they were standing out in the open. "I'm going to step back on my right foot and you step into my space with your left foot forward and tap down with your right foot at the same time."

Caroline tried to catch on. She placed both her hands on his shoulders to give herself room to look down at his feet.

"All right, now we tap three times in place and reverse the same steps." Jack wanted her back close against him. He wanted more than that.... "Only you have to move your hips a little. Let the music take over."

Caroline did her best to let the music fill her head, but there wasn't much room for music. Her thoughts were on Jack, on the feel of him, being held by him. He was an aphrodisiac to her system, blocking out everything else.

Jack put his hands to her hips and rotated her slowly as he brought her nearer. Caroline took the one step she needed to bring her body flush against his. Her hands came up to loop around his neck, and Jack lost it then. His control shattered. He lost sight of their surroundings. He lost sight of everything but Caroline in his arms.

"Caroline..." He said her name so softly she could barely hear it. But his heat and hardness spoke for itself.

Barely breathing, Caroline lifted her head to see his face. Her eyelids closed even before his head descended. It seemed to Caroline that it took aeons until Jack's mouth found hers. This was their first full kiss. It was a long-awaited kiss and timid at the start. But not for long. Their lips opened wider. Their tongues joined.

She was eager and fervent, secure and sure of herself. He was ravenous and passionate. He took one hand from her hip to ride it up beneath her jacket to the bare shoulder Gallagher had claimed. Jack's touch was possessive, and Caroline welcomed it with a low moan.

Jack kissed the base of her neck. Caroline moaned again and tightened her arms around his back. With a groan, Jack slid his other hand inside her jacket. Caroline swayed as Jack's palms rested just under her breasts while the earth quaked beneath her feet.

Caroline's mouth opened up even more invitingly to Jack's. Their teeth clashed, and their tongues and their lips. Jack's hands explored, caressing, stroking, thrilling. Caroline kissed his neck, his jaw, and then found her way back to his mouth. She put a hand inside his tuxedo jacket. Two more rhinestone studs slipped from his shirt as she sought to touch his chest. Ecstatically, Caroline discovered that Jack's heart was hammering as strenuously as hers.

"I want to make love to you," Jack breathed raggedly, tasting the corner of her swollen lips with the tip of his tongue. "We're going to be so good together. We understand each other."

"What do we understand?" Caroline asked dazedly.

"You don't have to worry about complications with me." Jack's voice was unsteady. "I don't want complications any more than you do."

Jack kissed Caroline again fully, and she responded with equal hunger.

Neither Caroline nor Jack heard the car pull up. They didn't hear the car door open. They didn't hear the footsteps approach.

"Okay, you two. Let's break it up." The police officer swung a flashlight in their faces.

Startled, Caroline and Jack sprang apart. Caroline was shaking. She had to hold on to Jack's arm for support. It took Jack a second before he had his wits about him.

Not wanting to be too hard on them, the officer turned the beam of his flashlight to the ground.

"Caroline, go sit in the car," Jack said fixedly, wanting to spare her any further discomfort. "I'll talk to the officer."

Caroline was red in the face as she looked from Jack to the officer, and it was not an agreeable kind of heat.

The officer nodded. "You can get in the car."

Jack opened the passenger door of his car for Caroline and whispered, "Roll the windows up." He didn't want her to hear anything that might embarrass her further, not that he wasn't embarrassed himself. He couldn't believe he'd been kissing her the way he'd been kissing her in the middle of the Long Island Expressway. But she did make him nuts enough to lose his head.

Dutifully, Caroline reached across her seat to roll up Jack's window, and then she rolled up hers. She sat huddled, shivering a little, sneaking peaks out at Jack and the officer. She saw Jack hand over his license and registration.

"I don't think there's a regulation on the books for this one," the officer said, struggling not to grin. Young himself, Officer Ed Van Cura knew how easy he melted when he was with his girlfriend. "Think you can get wherever you're going without pulling off the road again?"

Jack nodded. "Thanks for letting me get her in the car."

After a glance at the Toyota's front plate, Ed Van Cura gave Jack back his license and registration and moseyed over to his blue and white. The guys at the station house were going to get a kick out of this one.

Jack inhaled a deep cooling breath and got into the driver's side of the Toyota.

Caroline was looking straight ahead as Jack pulled out onto the expressway.

After being quiet for a few minutes, Jack said, "I'm sorry about that."

Caroline turned her head to Jack. "Which part are you sorry about?"

Jack thought about it a second. "The interruption," he answered with his comic instinct coming to the fore.

One look at Jack with a teasing grin on his face, and Caroline dissolved in giggles. Then Jack was joining her, roaring.

"What did the officer say?" Caroline asked, still laughing.

"Not much. I think he was even more embarrassed than we were." Jack chuckled. "I told him that you had me so unhinged that half the time I don't know where I'm at."

"Did you get a ticket?" Caroline smiled.

"There isn't a law on the books against kissing on the expressway." Jack grinned. "Not that I haven't already gotten a ticket on your account."

"That one wasn't my fault," Caroline quipped.

"This one would have been," Jack returned with a bedeviling smile.

"How do you figure that?" Caroline's eyes sparkled.

"I just told you that I don't think straight around you." This time the levity was gone from Jack's voice.

"I like that idea," Caroline whispered.

"Figured you might." Jack reached for her hand and held it.

Unavoidably, Caroline started wondering where all this was going to lead. Words that Jack had uttered in the heat of passion refiltered through Caroline's head. "Jack, when we were kissing, did you say something about there not being any complications?"

Jack nodded and smiled.

"What did you mean exactly?" Caroline queried.

"Just that we may both be through with love, but there isn't any reason that we can't get the best out of an attraction. It's such a plus to care without feeling threatened."

"I see." Caroline began to chew her tender bottom lip.

Jack smiled. "I never realized before how good it would feel to be perfectly honest with a woman. It's great that we think alike. Neither one of us has to worry about each other playing any mind games."

"Just great . . ." So, he wanted an affair—nothing permanent, nothing complicated—just a fling. Was that what she wanted?

Caroline felt the fire that Jack had created surge in her. She did want him. She wanted to be his. And she wanted him to be hers . . . all hers.

Jack glanced over at Caroline. She'd been quiet for some time now. The cassette tape of Latin dance music came to an end. Jack exchanged it for a tape of instrumental rhythm and blues. He noticed a motel off to his left. But he didn't want to take her to any "no tell" motel. He wanted to take her to his apartment. Only he couldn't just drive her to his apartment without some preliminary discussion. She'd have to let Myra know she was spending the night out.

Caroline snuck a look at Jack as he checked his sideview mirror. She just wasn't as sophisticated as he thought she was. She was old-fashioned and romantic. She wanted love. She wanted forever after.

Jack was waiting for a sign from Caroline so that he would know exactly how to proceed. He wondered if he should mention that he didn't want to settle for an hour or two with her. Of course, he would settle if he had to. They could always make plans for the future. He thought of the possibility of taking her away for an entire weekend. He liked that idea a lot.

"Are you okay?" he asked, giving her one of his dynamic soft looks. He noted that she seemed a trifle uneasy.

"I'm fine." She really would have liked to explain to him what was going on in her head, but she hadn't sorted it out herself yet. He was right about her not wanting any complication in her life, but she didn't think she wanted a fling. She didn't know what she wanted. . . .

Jack didn't think her "I'm fine" sounded very convincing, and as he studied her again, she looked to him like she was more than uneasy. She looked scared to death. Did she think he wouldn't be gentle with her, adoring, and tender?

"Caroline?" Jack cleared an emotional frog from his throat.

"What?" Her tone bristled in the still air of the car.

Jack wanted a sign from her, but not the sign she was giving him now. She was looking straight ahead, deliberately avoiding his eyes. He wanted her back the way she was when she was in his arms, kissing him with as much desire as he'd been kissing her.

"Nothing," Jack said after a few beats. He was more a man of action than a talker. They were almost at the house, and as soon as he was able to stop the car he'd reassure her the best way possible when he took her into his arms. Then they could work out the details for the balance of the night.

Jack stepped harder on the gas, but kept an eye out for the highway patrol.

Caroline didn't even give Jack a chance to turn the motor off as he pulled into the driveway. Before Jack even knew what was happening, Caroline had released the lock on her door and pushed it open.

In bewilderment, Jack watched her step out.

"Thanks for everything," Caroline said, bending to talk to him in the car. "I had a really good time." She flapped a hand nervously and then closed the door.

Dumbfounded, Jack watched Caroline race up the stairs of the porch and then quickly let herself into the house. She didn't turn her head to him even once.

Jack covered his face with his hands and then banged his forehead on the steering wheel. Of all the plans he'd made for himself for the remainder of the night, not once had he considered the possibility of going home to take a cold shower.

Chapter Nine

"Well, look who's here," Billy D'Anriolli called out as Jack, in gray shorts and a denim shirt with the sleeves cut off, walked onto the basketball court.

Jack nodded warmly to Eddie Ruiz, Philly Tormaine and Billy D. He'd been friends with the three of them since high school. They were all the same age, give or take a half calendar of months. It had been a long time since he'd been over to the park on a Sunday morning in the old neighborhood. He hadn't fully realized until now how much he'd missed the guys. They'd all tried in turns to nudge him out of his funk, stopping by the yard, calling him up, but he'd needed to make the move on his own. He'd decided that it was about time he reentered the world.

"Thought you had forgotten about us." Philly flashed expressive brown eyes. Philly, rangy and lean with dark brown hair cut short to keep it from curling, was the agitator of the group. His remarks were sometimes cutting, but there wasn't any bite intended. He'd be the first to take the shirt off his back for any one of them.

"He invited us to the wedding, didn't he?" Bandying, Billy D. put in a good word as he turned the brim of the baseball cap he was wearing from front to back. As usual, Billy D.'s face still held the shadow of a heavy beard though he'd shaved close. He often joked that when his hair was gone completely—it was already receding—he'd grow a beard and wrap it around his head.

"Didn't you hear?" Philly ribbed. "That's why she called it off. Jilly couldn't stand the idea of seeing any of us in the church or the reception, especially you. I think she was afraid you'd take up more than one seat."

With a smirk, Billy D. looked down at himself. At six foot two, Billy D. was built like a weight lifter on hiatus. There was a meal or two extra around his gut. Sucking in deeply, Billy D. flattened his stomach against the press of his hand. "I don't know, guys. Do you think this is why I haven't made detective yet?"

"Nah," Philly joked. "You haven't made detective yet because you're too dumb to pass the test."

They all laughed, including Billy D., who then rebutted, "If you guys remember back to high school, I got the highest grade of all of you on the math regents."

"That's because you have that extra toe on your left foot to count with," Eddie joshed, elevating the horseplay. Eddie, as hyper as ever, kept in motion by dribbling a basketball. The light blue shirt he'd left opened over his cutoff jeans flapped as he zig-zagged, exposing his firmly muscled chest. His girlfriend Sue called him "Animal," but she always said it with love. Eddie often took heat from the guys over the nickname.

"What have you been doing with yourself?" Jack directed the question to Eddie.

"Philly got me into selling insurance with him," Eddie said with a sigh. "I guess it's better than selling shoes."

"And it isn't as dirty as being an auto mechanic," Philly added with double meaning.

They all remembered when Eddie had taken a job as an auto mechanic right after high school and how riled he'd gotten when the owner of the garage wanted him to pad the bill of a little old lady.

Jack recalled that day especially well. He'd happened by to see if Eddie wanted to go for lunch and had been just in time to keep Eddie from jamming his fist down his boss's throat.

Jack smiled. "I thought I was next on the list and that you were going to come in with me and Ray."

Eddie grinned, slicing his dark hair from his face with one hand. "It's first come, first serve. And you weren't around when I'd had it working in real estate. I still say I should have tried becoming a male dancer that time I got propositioned." Fooling around, Eddie gyrated his hips.

Billy D. poked Jack as he responded to Eddie. "Yeah, Animal, you should have, and when Sue got through with you, you'd be walking funny for the rest of your life."

"How did I get to be the butt here?" Eddie complained, grinning. "Shouldn't we all be on Jackson's case?"

"You're right," Philly agreed, focusing on Jack.

Jack smiled genially. He knew he had it coming. "Go easy with me. I'm still delicate."

Eddie tossed Jack the ball. His gold ID bracelet, a gift from Sue, glinted on his right hand. "Yeah, but I hear you're maneuvering again. Sue told me about the fox you were with in La Casa not too long ago. The one who gave you a shiner."

"A shiner... This I've got to hear." Billy D. beat Philly to the punch.

"There's nothing to tell." Trying to duck a conversation about Caroline, Jack shot for the hoop. He'd already had a conversation about her with himself when he'd first gotten up in the morning. And he'd allowed, after thoughtful consideration, that what hadn't happened the night before between them was just as well. In fact, he'd come to the conclusion that the smartest thing he could do was stop hassling himself by being around her. He didn't need the frustration or the aggravation.

"Come on, Jackson." Philly chased Jack around on the court. "We want to hear about your shiner. The least you can do is let the three of us live vicariously."

"Hey, I'm still living," Eddie refuted Philly. "It's only you and Billy D. who are married. Me, I'm still a free agent."

Philly laughed. "You'd better not let Sue hear that."

It hit Jack without any associated enthusiasm that he was really the only free agent of the group, including Ray. Did he really want to go from woman to woman seeking intimacy in small doses? Was Ray right? Was he afraid to lead with his heart?

"When are you and Sue going to name the day?" Jack worked on redirecting the focus.

"We're saving up," Eddie answered. "I think we're almost there, providing we don't kill each other first. Last night I said to her, 'Baby, I don't even have enough money to buy food from the allowance you're giving me.' She said, 'Come to La Casa every night for dinner and my mother and father will feed you.'"

Philly winked at Billy D. before speaking to Eddie. "Your mistake was letting her open up a joint account. If you don't train them right before you're married, you're doomed."

Eddie retorted. "So how much allowance does Lisa give you?"

Philly grinned. "Before I beg or after?"

"Is that the trick?" Eddie laughed.

Philly shook his head. "Nah, it never works."

"Speaking of food," Billy D. chimed in, "I think we should walk over to the diner and get some breakfast. And I think Jackson should spring for it."

Jack smiled. "All right, but did you, at least, eat once already this morning?"

"Just coffee," was Philly D.'s rejoinder. "My in-laws came over."

Two girls in skinny shorts and midriff tops jogged by the court, reminding the four men of the girls they'd all chased back in high school.

"Jailbait," Billy D. groaned.

"You're lucky that Diana isn't around to catch you looking," Eddie chuckled.

Billy D. contradicted him. "I have Diana's permission to look as long as I wipe the drool from my chin before she sees it."

Jack felt suddenly despondent listening to Philly, Eddie and Billy D. teasing about the women in their lives. Philly had been happily married to Lisa for twelve years now, having bit the bullet a year out of high school. He had three kids already. All boys. Billy D. and Diana had gotten married two years ago, and they still behaved like honeymooners. Eddie sidetracked now and then, but there wasn't any doubt in anyone's mind, least of all Sue's, that she and Eddie were a foregone conclusion. And then there was Ray and Gloria. Jack knew it was just a matter of time before they took the plunge. How was it that some found the secret and others never did?

"Hey, Jackson, where'd you go?" Eddie snapped his fingers in front of Jack's face, penetrating Jack's reverie.

"Right here," Jack smiled, forcing it.

"Well, give me the ball," Eddie said. "I want to throw it in my trunk and then we can go to the diner."

Jack bounced the ball to Eddie, and Eddie volleyed with it as they walked to the parking lot.

"I'm going to have to eat and run," Philly said when they got to Eddie's car. "I'm taking the boys to a carnival this afternoon so that Lisa can have some time to herself."

"Where's the carnival?" Jack asked, a spontaneous idea forming in his head. Of course, it was only there for a moment before he was second-guessing himself.

I thought you were going to stay away from her.

I am staying away from her. What's the big deal in asking her and the kids to spend the afternoon at a carnival? I'm only thinking about the kids.

Liar...

"It's over at the Knights of Columbus grounds on Eighty-sixth Street," Philly answered as they headed for the diner.

"Hey, Eddie," Jack said, smiling. "How would you like to switch cars with me for the day?"

Looking shocked, Eddie stopped walking. "You're going to let me have your MR2 so that you can drive my Buick? What am I, dreaming? I didn't think you even let Ray behind the wheel of your car."

"You'd better say yes before I change my mind," Jack warned.

"Why don't you ask me?" Philly interjected.

"You won't be able to fit three kids in my car," Jack explained. And he needed a back seat for Caroline's kids.

"The answer is yes." Eddie quickly threw Jack his car keys before Billy D. got into the act. "The registration is in my glove compartment."

Jack took his car keys off his key chain and pulled his registration from his wallet. He handed both over to Eddie. "I'll catch up with you either tonight or sometime tomorrow. I hope you have insurance on yourself, because if you so much as get it scratched, you're going to need it."

Eddie grinned. "I've got insurance. How do you think I made commission my first week?"

"Let's get to the diner if we're going," Billy D. grumbled, sorry he hadn't been fast enough to get involved in the car exchange.

With a bathrobe on over her pajamas, Caroline carried a platter of pancakes and a container of milk from the back kitchen door to the blanket she'd spread out on the grass behind the house. Giggling, Elizabeth and Bobby, also in robes, followed after their mother, each holding breakfast fixings. Myra had declined Caroline's invitation to the picnic. Sitting at the kitchen table, she sipped her coffee, munched toast, and read Sunday's Long Island *Newsday*.

"I don't think anyone has a Mom as silly as you," Elizabeth said, enjoying her mother's plan.

"But we still love you, Mom, even if you have nutty ideas," Bobby added.

"Are you two calling me silly and nutty?" Caroline exclaimed with feigned chagrin as she placed the platter of pancakes and milk down in the center of the blanket.

"Yes, we are," Bobby confirmed, putting down plates, forks and cups while Elizabeth set down a bottle of maple syrup and butter.

Caroline widened her eyes. "I'm going to have to get the two of you for that."

Bobby rocked on his slippered feet. "You have to catch us first." Copying her brother, Elizabeth ran when Bobby ran.

Caroline chased them around the backyard and wound up romping with both of them on the grass. Sputtering as she laughed, Caroline said, "Now, come on and let's eat before the pancakes get cold."

The three took places on the blanket. Caroline served.

"Are you sure you didn't put any wheat germ in this time?" Bobby questioned suspiciously.

"Did you see any wheat germ out when I was cooking?" Caroline asked, evading him neatly. Not only had she used wheat germ, she'd also made them with soymilk, which was another health-food item her kids objected to.

Bobby wasn't convinced. "You had it all mixed before we came downstairs."

Elizabeth put butter and syrup on her helping and tasted it gingerly. "There's no germs, Bobby," she assured her brother. "You know I can taste it when there's germs. These are the best pancakes ever."

Taking his sister's word, Bobby spread butter and syrup on his pancakes, and after taking a sample, began to wolf them down.

Smiling to herself, Caroline poured milk for the three of them. She'd already had two cups of coffee. "What time will the Robertsons be picking the two of you up?" She'd given permission for the Robertsons to take Elizabeth and Bobby on a day's outing to Montauk with their two kids, a boy and a girl the same age as Elizabeth and Bobby. And since the kids had plans, Caroline had made plans for herself to take in a matinee in the city with Stacy.

Bobby answered, "About one o'clock. Kevin said he was going to call me first."

"Mommy," Elizabeth spoke wistfully. "Do you like Jack Corey?"

"Well..." Caroline got flushed. She'd been making a concerted effort not to even think about him. "Did you like him?" Caroline asked instead of answering.

Elizabeth nodded her head, her mouth full at the moment.

Caroline ate some of her pancakes.

"Bobby, did you like him?" Elizabeth asked after she'd swallowed.

"He's okay. I guess." Coming from Bobby, that was a rave endorsement.

Elizabeth looked back at her mother. "Is he your boyfriend?"

"My what?" Caroline gulped her milk.

"Is he your boyfriend?" Elizabeth repeated innocently.

"Well, he's sort of a friend, but not a boyfriend," Caroline answered uncomfortably, fighting not to let herself get worked up over Jack Corey. She had his number. He'd given it to her. The louse... She probably wasn't even his only game in town....

"If he's a friend and he's a boy, then he's a boyfriend." Elizabeth counted that analysis off on two fingers. "And if he kisses you, it's for sure. Did he?"

"It doesn't quite work that way with grown-ups," Caroline said, circumventing her daughter.

Elizabeth didn't let go. "How does it work?"

Caroline glanced over at Bobby. For the first time that Caroline could remember she was hoping Bobby would say something to annoy his sister. But Bobby was munching away, listening intently to the discussion.

"Grown-ups look for relationships. That's the difference," Caroline responded. On the bright side, she was relieved that she didn't have to deal with the complexity of compatibility where Jack was concerned. Nor did she have to worry about how long it would take for him to get tired of her and her jinxes.

"What's a relationship?" Elizabeth was not quelled.

Caroline pictured herself on the phone with Dr. Ruth. *Isn't seven years old too young for the facts of life?*

"A relationship..." Caroline began haltingly. "A relationship is when two people want to spend time together. They think about each other. They do nice things for each other. They laugh a lot. They make each other feel better when they're sad. They do more than kiss. It's something that comes from the heart."

"Do you know when you first meet a boy that he's going to be your boyfriend?" Elizabeth questioned while she ate.

"Not right away. You have to get to know each other first." Caroline smiled, pleased with her answer.

"Maybe Mr. Corey will be your boyfriend later," Elizabeth said thoughtfully as she finished her pancakes.

"Well...well," Caroline repeated, having trouble coming up with a resolution this time. "There has to be a sort of feeling right from the start. It's hard to explain. It's called attraction." Caroline fanned herself with a napkin, suddenly feeling quite warm.

"Elizabeth, you don't know anything about boyfriends," Bobby jeered, having finally had enough of this mushy talk.

Elizabeth stuck up for herself. "That's 'cause I'm too young. And when I do have a boyfriend, I'm not going to tell you."

Bobby gave Elizabeth a crooked smile. "Like I care. You're probably never going to have a boyfriend, anyway."

"I will too if I want to. . . ."

Caroline neutralized the scene. "I think it's time we all went in and got dressed. The Robertsons may want to leave earlier, and I have to get going. Now, each of you take your dishes to the sink."

Giving each other nasty looks, Elizabeth and Bobby picked up their dishes and silverware and got up from the blanket. As soon as the kids walked into the kitchen from the back door, Caroline splashed what was left of her cold milk on her face and then blotted herself with a wad of napkins. The attraction she couldn't explain had given her an entire body flush.

Jack dialed Caroline's number from his apartment. He'd showered again and changed into brown slacks and a beige polo shirt replete with a designer logo. Eddie's car was parked outside.

Elizabeth answered on the first ring. "Hello. This is Elizabeth."

"Hi, Elizabeth. This is Jack Corey. Can I speak to your mother?"

"She's not home."

In the background, Jack heard Myra say, "Elizabeth, give me the phone.

"Hello." Myra's voice came through the receiver. "Who's calling?"

"Hi, Myra. It's Jack Corey. When will Caroline be back?"

"Not till this evening. She went into the city to meet a friend and take in a matinee. Her friend Stacy." Myra added the last not wanting Jack to think Caroline was meeting a man.

Jack could hardly believe how disappointed he felt. "Well..."

"Is there something I can tell her when she gets home?"

"No, I was just calling to see if she and the kids wanted to go to a carnival this afternoon?"

"Oh, what a shame." Myra tisked. "Elizabeth and Bobby were supposed to go to Montauk with friends, but Bobby's friend took sick. The family called after Caroline left. Right now they're going crazy because they don't have anything to do, and I think I'm coming down with something. Caroline is going to be sorry she missed your call. I know that she and the kids would have loved to go to a carnival."

"What carnival?" Bobby asked loudly. "Can we go?"

"You can't go because your mother is not home," Myra responded to Bobby.

"Mommy would let us go," Elizabeth whined.

Myra came back on the line with Jack. "I know I'm going to hear about this all day."

"I want to call my mother and ask her," Elizabeth said behind Myra and loud enough for Jack to hear.

"You can't call your mother," Myra answered.

"I'm really sorry I got them going," Jack apologized.

"I don't suppose..." Myra cut herself off.

"Well..." Jack knew what Myra was about to suggest. He had planned this for the kids, hadn't he? "Caroline might not like the idea...." He didn't think he was particularly keen on it himself.

"I'm sure it would be all right with Caroline." Myra turned her mouth from the receiver. "Elizabeth, Bobby,

Mr. Corey is going to take the two of you. Isn't that nice?''

Jack heard two sappy sequels. Wait a minute... What did he know about kids? "I'll pick them up in about an hour.''

"They'll be ready.'' Myra wet the tip of her forefinger and held it in the air. Strike one up for Cupid Myra. And besides, she really was coming down with something.

"Great.'' Jack hoped he hadn't bitten off more than he could chew.

Caroline got home at 6:00 p.m. She called out to Myra and then followed her voice upstairs, where she found the housekeeper lying in bed in her room, looking green around the gills.

Caroline rushed over to Myra's bed. "Do you need a doctor?''

"No, it's just a stomach virus. It will probably be over in twenty-four hours.''

"How about some tea? Or a cold compress for your head?'' Caroline was concerned.

"I don't want anything. All I've been doing is sleeping on and off. I just want to sleep.''

Caroline nodded. "All right, but just call me if you want anything?''

"I will.''

"Did the Robertsons say what time they'd be bringing the kids home?'' Caroline asked on her way to the door.

"They're not with the Robertsons. One of their kids got sick and they called it off.''

"Where are Bobby and Elizabeth?''

"At the carnival.''

"What carnival? Who did they go with?''

"Jack Corey. He called to ask if you and the kids wanted to go to a carnival. The kids got all excited when they heard me talking to him about it. I guess he didn't want to disappoint them, so he agreed to take them without you. I didn't think you'd mind."

Caroline did mind. Elizabeth and Bobby were bound to think that there was more going on than there was. That was just what she needed after this morning's conversation.

Myra lifted herself up from her pillow. "You don't mind that he took them, do you?"

"No," Caroline lied. She didn't want to upset Myra. "Did he say what time he'd be bringing them home?" Exactly what was she going to tell Elizabeth and Bobby when he stopped coming around?

"I don't think he said, but they should be home soon." Myra rolled onto her stomach.

"I'm going downstairs to wait for them, but call if you need me."

"I will."

Caroline walked out of Myra's bedroom and then continued downstairs to wait. Angry with Jack, Caroline paced the living room. In the middle of her second rotation, she heard a car pull up.

Caroline was waiting in the foyer when the door opened. Bobby was the first in the house, followed by Jack who was carrying Elizabeth. "What happened?" Caroline rushed forward, all alarmed. She tried to pry Elizabeth from Jack's arms.

"Mommy, I'm sick," Elizabeth answered, tenaciously holding on to Jack's neck.

"Why don't I get her up to her bedroom and then you can look her over?" Jack suggested. "She doesn't seem to have a fever, but her stomach hurts. She just started to complain about it."

"We didn't eat any junk," Bobby insisted, walking behind his mother who was walking right behind Jack and Elizabeth as they climbed the stairs.

Elizabeth began to cry. "I think I'm going to throw up."

They were in the upstairs hall right in front of Caroline's bedroom. Jack made a dash with Elizabeth to Caroline's bathroom. Caroline ran with him. Ready to gag at the prospect of seeing his sister vomit, Bobby scooted off for his bedroom and quickly shut his door.

Elizabeth threw up partially on Jack, partially on Caroline and partially in the bathroom sink. She was crying hysterically. Jack crooned to her as he turned the water on with one hand. "It's okay. Let it come up." Caroline ran a towel under the water and held it to her daughter's temple. "Jack is right," Caroline concurred. "Honey, let it all up."

"I don't have anymore," Elizabeth whimpered.

Caroline wiped Elizabeth's face with the towel and then bent down to press her palm to Elizabeth's forehead, checking her for any sign of fever. Jack stood by, watching Elizabeth's bottom lip quiver. He hadn't noticed until now how much Elizabeth resembled her mother. Caroline's bottom lip had quivered in the same cute way the day she'd messed her hair up.

"I'll put her in bed," Caroline told Jack as she guided Elizabeth away.

Jack went down to the kitchen and found scouring powder and a sponge, then went back upstairs to Caroline's bathroom to clean the sink. Once he'd finished, he took his designer polo shirt off and rinsed it. After ringing it out, he brought it downstairs to the dryer. He was sitting at the kitchen table straddling a chair when Caroline came downstairs barefoot, looking cuddly in a pink terry robe.

"She really didn't eat any junk," Jack repeated. "She seemed fine all day, then the next thing I knew she was sick."

Caroline stood with her hip pressed to the kitchen sink, her arms folded akimbo. She could hear the dryer going as she noted Jack's bare chest. "Myra is down with a virus. Elizabeth probably picked it up the same time Myra did."

Jack felt relieved that Caroline wasn't going to blame him for getting Elizabeth sick... But why did she look like she was ready to kill him?

"Listen, I'm sorry, anyway," he said for good measure.

"You don't have to apologize. You didn't get her sick," Caroline said tightly.

Hmm, Jack said to himself. He was definitely in trouble, here.

"Would you like some tea?" Caroline asked aloofly, marshaling herself before she let him have it.

"Sure." Jack examined her. Unless he was mistaken, something was very wrong here. "Did you have dinner?"

"I had a large lunch." Caroline filled the kettle and brought it to the stove.

"If you have some eggs, I could whip us up some omelets." Jack figured he'd try a domestic approach as he already felt a domestic ambience with her in a robe, cooking, while he sat at the table.

"No, thank you," Caroline replied stiffly, waiting impatiently for the dryer to stop so that she could send him on his way with his shirt on.

"Are you going to tell me what's bothering you?" Jack found himself talking to her back.

Caroline turned to him. She had her hands on her hips. "I don't want you getting to know my kids, and I don't want them getting to know you."

Jack got up from his chair and came up to her. They stood in the middle of the kitchen, squaring off in a manner more suited to two boxers than potential lovers.

"Why not?"

The bell on the dryer rang.

It was hard for Caroline to concentrate with his chest in her face. "Could you put your shirt on?"

"You tell me why you don't want me getting to know your kids and then I'll put my shirt on." He was not going to lose any ground by walking away. "We really had a good time together."

"That's all the more reason," Caroline said tightly. "I don't want to have to explain to them why you're not coming around when you're not coming around anymore. That's why."

"What?" Jack thought he might need a road map to figure that one out.

"I am not going to have a fling with you." Caroline lowered the boom on him.

Jack was floored. "A fling? Is that what you think we're having?"

"If it's not a fling, then what is it?" She stared at him, feeling all vulnerable but refusing to show it.

Agitated, Jack ran his fingers through his hair. "I don't know what we're having. Half of the time I'm around you, I don't even know what I'm doing.... Make that three-quarters of the time. No, make that most of the time."

Caroline didn't appreciate his tone of voice. "Who said you have to be around me?"

"No one." Jack hiked to the utility room for his shirt. He walked back waving it at her. It was too hot to put on, though it was hardly much different from his own body temperature. "Tell Elizabeth I hope she feels better." With that last remark, Jack walked out the front door and slammed it on his way out.

Caroline was even more upset after Jack walked out. She hadn't meant for him to get angry with her. She'd only meant to get angry with him.

Chapter Ten

Elizabeth was herself again by the next morning and insisted on going to school. Caroline conceded after watching her eat a full breakfast. After the kids left on the school bus, Caroline threw herself fully into house cleaning. She refused to let Myra do even the simplest of chores. With her hands occupied, it was easier for Caroline not to think about whether or not Marty would call today with a job. And keeping busy helped a little to exorcise thoughts about Jack.

"Elizabeth told me that she and Bobby had a great time at the carnival with Jack," Myra commented, seated at the kitchen table. "The more I get to know Jack, the more I get to like him."

Her back up, Caroline smelled inside a bowl that had been covered with wrap. She wished she knew the right buttons to press that would make Jack see that she could be more than a possible plaything. She could be likable, too.

"Elizabeth was upset that she'd thrown up on him," Myra continued. "It's just as well that he's getting a firsthand lesson on what it's like to be around kids."

"Why is it just as well?" Caroline asked, showing annoyance. But she was immediately contrite that she was taking her rotten disposition out on Myra. Closing the refrigerator, Caroline leaned up against the door. "I'm sorry, Myra. I didn't mean to snap. It's just that I know what you're thinking. You're thinking that he's looking to make a commitment. But he isn't. He told me he isn't."

"All men find it difficult to make a commitment. It was the same in my day. I think they all just sort of glide into it without realizing. My mother used to say to me that a woman chases a man until he catches her. Of course, that was before women's lib. I don't think things have changed that much."

Caroline scowled. "Are you telling me to chase after him?"

"If you've fallen in love with him, you will."

Caroline felt her breathing change and her body go all shaky. "I won't deny that I'm attracted to him, but that's all it is, and I don't intend to act on it."

The phone rang, startling both women. Caroline raced to pick the receiver up.

"Hello," she said quickly, stupidly hoping it was Jack as much as she was hoping it was Marty.

"Caroline?"

The voice was male, but it wasn't Marty or Jack.

"Yes," Caroline responded.

"Hi, it's Ray Sanchez. Jack's brother."

"Oh, hi." Caroline was surprised to hear from him. Was Ray calling because something had happened to Jack? Caroline gripped the receiver tighter.

"I'm throwing a party tonight for Gloria. It's her birthday. I know Gloria would really like it if you could come."

"I..." Caroline faltered. "I'd really love to come, but..."

"Do you have other plans for this evening?"

"No." Caroline nervously tapped her fingers on the countertop. "I suppose Jack will be there...."

"Sure." Ray took an educated guess why Caroline was hesitant. "Don't tell me that my brother took his foul mood out on you last night? I was hoping he was just not himself this morning."

Caroline's mouth was dry. She knew it was likely that she was responsible for Jack's lousy mood. And she had another thought.... "Is he with you now?"

"No, he's out on a job. So, will you come? It's very informal. Just a small group of close friends. And I promise I'll keep my brother away from you if he hasn't gotten his act together by then. Listen, it's at eight o'clock. Let me give you my address and directions and you can decide by then. Do you have something to write on?"

There was a pad and pencil on the counter. "Yes... But I really don't think I'll be able to make it. I really wish I could." She was consciously making a decision not to be around Jack. He played too much havoc with her senses.

"If we see you, we see you," Ray said, and then gave his address and directions as Caroline wrote.

"What was that all about?" Myra asked after Caroline hung up.

"It was Jack's brother Ray. He's having a birthday party for his girlfriend tonight, and he asked me to come. Gloria, that's his girlfriend, is very nice, and we really hit it off. I told you about her, didn't I? I met her at Jack's mother's apartment."

"Yes, you mentioned her." Myra was giving Caroline a close look. "Why don't you want to go?"

"I'm fairly sure that Jack would rather I didn't go." Caroline put her palm in the air defensively. "Don't ask me why."

Myra sighed, but wisely kept her mouth closed.

Caroline, filled with nervous apprehension, rang the doorbell at Ray's apartment at a quarter after eight. She did like Gloria. But that wasn't the only reason she'd finally talked herself into coming. Try as she might, Caroline couldn't resist making an attempt to see if she and Jack couldn't at least be friends...not that she didn't wonder if she was just kidding herself.

Ray answered the door. "Great. You made it." He was all smiles as he ushered her in.

Caroline was able to see into the living room from the hallway. There were four men in the living room having a heated conversation as they sat on stools around a corner bar. Jack was not one of them. As best she could tell, Jack was not in the room.

"Do you want to take your jacket off?" Ray asked.

"Okay." Caroline slipped out of her wool blazer, shifting her black shoulder bag from arm to arm and the small gift-wrapped box she was holding from hand to hand. She wondered where Jack was. She wondered where Gloria was. And were there going to be other women?

"You look terrific," Ray said after hanging Caroline's jacket in the hall closet.

"Thanks." Caroline smiled. She wore black flats, and a gray turtleneck under a red silk blouse. They were tucked into a mid-calf-length gray wool skirt and cinched together with a wide black leather belt. She'd changed clothes so many times she had to look down at herself to remember what she was wearing.

"Gloria is in the kitchen with the gals," Ray explained. "They're fussing with the cold cuts and salads. Gloria didn't like my presentation. I thought the salads were fine in their containers. And I don't know what was wrong with just sticking all the cold cuts together on a tray. I separated them, sort of. Come on, I'll bring you into the kitchen and then you can meet the guys."

The guys paused in their conversation to check Caroline out as Ray walked her through the living room. Caroline wondered again where Jack was. Hadn't he come? Was he in the kitchen?

Gloria looked up as Ray and Caroline came into the kitchen. She'd just finished jelly-rolling slices of roast beef. Wiping her hands on the apron around her waist, Gloria rushed over.

"I'm so glad you came." Gloria gave Caroline a big hug.

"Happy birthday," Caroline said warmly, handing Gloria the gift she was holding.

"Thanks. I'll open it later with the others."

"Hi." Sue Conway walked up.

"Hi, Sue." Caroline smiled.

Gloria wanted to know how Caroline and Sue knew each other.

"Jack took me to La Casa one night." Caroline recalled how much fun they'd had. Maybe Jack would remember that night and give her some points.

"Do you want me to carry anything out?" Ray asked.

"We'll bring it all out in just a few minutes. Did Jack get back from the bakery?"

Ray shook his head. "I still don't know how I could have forgotten to get rolls and bread. I mean, I was there getting the cake."

Gloria smiled. "Nina has already told me that if your head wasn't attached you'd forget it somewhere."

Ray's dark eyes gleamed with laughter. "How do you like that? I've got a mother who cuts me down. What else did she tell you?"

"I'll tell you later. I don't want to embarrass you." Gloria gave Ray a loving peck on his cheek. "Now, go inside. We'll be out with the food in a minute."

"Is there anything I can do?" Caroline asked after Ray left.

"We're done," Gloria answered. "We were just gossiping. Let me introduce you." Gloria brought Caroline over to the kitchen table. "This is Lisa Tormaine, Diana D'Anriolli, and Genna Reeves. Everybody, Caroline Phelps."

Caroline, who had been concerned about her attire for more than one reason, felt relaxed that she was appropriately dressed. Gloria was wearing a skirt and blouse, as was Sue. The other women all wore nice slacks and sweaters.

Caroline shook hands with Lisa, a pretty girl with enormous brown eyes and short, curly dark hair. Caroline shook hands with Diana, who was obviously a natural redhead. Her eyebrows matched her hair color, and she had faint freckles across the bridge of her nose. And Caroline shook hands with Genna, a petite brunette with a peaches-and-cream complexion.

"Gloria and I try to catch your soap even when we're on duty at the hospital," Genna said. "We both tape it, as well."

Caroline smiled wanly. "My last scene should run the end of this week."

Gloria informed Lisa and Diana that Caroline was an actress.

"I didn't know you were a celebrity," Sue said, all animated.

Caroline was self-conscious. "I'm not a celebrity. I'm just a working girl who is currently out of work."

Jack walked into the kitchen carrying two large white paper bags. As soon as he saw Caroline, Jack's adrenaline kicked in. And as soon as Caroline saw Jack, her heart started palpitating.

"I didn't know that Ray had asked you over," Jack said, caught by surprise.

He looked unbelievably sexy in a slouchy green-and-tan-striped sweater and brown slacks.

"Well, yes. He did." Skittish, Caroline glanced away. Why hadn't Ray told Jack that he'd asked her to come? She could only assume that he hadn't because Jack would have objected.

Gloria was instantly aware that something was amiss. "I'll take the bread, Jack."

Jack, who had been standing stock-still, handed the two bags over. "Well..." he said to Caroline.

"Yes...well," Caroline responded, wanting to dash out the apartment door.

Gloria put the rolls in a bowl and the rye bread on a small platter. "Jack, could you take the cold cuts out?"

Caroline stared down at her feet. Jack picked up the tray of cold cuts and stalked out of the kitchen.

"What's going on?" Gloria asked.

Unstrung, Caroline made a hapless motion with her hand. "Going on? Nothing's going on."

"Oh, listen. I'm sorry. You don't have to talk about it if you don't want to."

"There just isn't anything to say." Caroline stood forlornly.

The other women gathered around, feeling a sense of rapport.

"I have an idea," Sue said. "Caroline, you stay in the kitchen. The rest of us will go into the living room and Gloria can send Jack back in for the rest of the food. That will give the two of you a few minutes alone."

A look of panic crossed Caroline's face. "No, really...that's not necessary." She wasn't up to being alone with Jack.

"Hey, ladies. Where's the bread and salads?" A husky voice called from the living room.

"That's Animal." Sue sighed and smiled.

Gloria put her arm around Caroline's shoulders. "Caroline, just don't leave. Okay? I know that Jack has feelings for you. Whatever is wrong right now will work itself out."

"I don't think so." Caroline knew Jack had some feelings for her. Just not the right feelings. "I'll stay... for a while." It would have been more humiliating to leave at this point.

Sue and the other three women picked up the rest of the food and exited the kitchen. Gloria and Caroline followed them out.

For the next hour everyone ate heartily except for Caroline and Jack, who only toyed with their food. The men hung together around the bar discussing sports. The women sat around talking fashion, TV and kids. Caroline and Jack tried to avoid each other's eyes. The other women, however, recorded a number of glances between Caroline and Jack that were intended to go by unnoticed.

"Hey, birthday girl," Ray said, coming over to drape his arm around Gloria. "Are you going to open your gifts or do you want the cake first?"

Gloria, looking especially radiant, smiled. "Let's save the cake till later."

Ray waved the men over. Caroline had a sudden desperate hope that Jack would come stand by her side. But he didn't. He stood with Sue and Eddie, leaving her to Lisa and Diana. He did flash his blue eyes her way once, but his expression was unreadable, and Caroline, struggling even harder to remain composed, looked away. Whatever had possessed her to think that they could at least be friends?

Gloria opened her gifts amid murmurs of approval. There were soft kid gloves from Diana and Billy. A beautiful hand-embroidered scarf from Lisa and Philly. Gloria opened a box with a lovely cream silk blouse, and Eddie said to Sue, "So that's what we bought." Genna and her fiancé, Tim Weston, gave Gloria a white wool cardigan. Their card read, *Now when you're cold at work, you'll still be in uniform.* Jack went to the closet where he'd hung his leather bomber jacket and came back with his gift. The necklace he'd chosen, a single crystal on a gold chain, gave Caroline a start. It was coincidentally a perfect match to the crystal earrings she'd purchased. Caroline was relieved that she'd guessed right and Gloria's ears were pierced.

"Wait a second here," Philly said with a Cheshire cat grin. "Ray, where's your gift?"

Ray had his hand in the pocket of his navy slacks. His eyes were on Gloria. "Do you think you guys could make a little room for me here?"

They all moved a little away from Gloria, who was sitting on a gray tweed couch in the center of the room. Ray got down on his knees in front of her.

"Wait a minute." It was Jack who halted the proceedings. "I have to get the camera." Going back to the hall closet, Jack returned with the video camera that he'd rented for this occasion.

"Set?" Ray sent Jack a glance.

"Ready." Jack nodded.

Gloria watched Ray with her eyes all aglow. She'd had a strong feeling that this was going to be the night. And she was ready for it.

Ray pulled a jeweller's ring box from his pocket. His hand was shaking.

"Gloria," Ray said humbly. "I know I can be a fool at times, forgetful and impossibly stubborn. I know that you'd like me to show my feelings more, even in public. Gloria, you deserve more than I can ever be. But no one will ever love you more than I do. I promise to love you and adore you for the rest of my life. I promise to take care of you and comfort you. I'm going to try hard to show my feelings more. I'm putting this all on tape for you so you can remind me if I ever slip. Gloria, will you please be my wife?"

"Oh, yes, Ray," Gloria whispered emotionally, her eyes all misty.

Ray opened the black velvet box. "Honey, someday I'll get you one that's a lot bigger."

Tears of joy ran down Gloria's cheeks. "Once you put this ring on my finger, Ray, it is never coming off."

Ray took Gloria's hand in his and adorned her finger with a delicate diamond ring. Gloria threw her arms around Ray. They kissed while Jack captured the moment for them on tape.

Jack panned the other faces in the room with the camera. His focus stayed long on Caroline with her unaware. He saw the tears glimmering in the corners of her beautiful hazel eyes. Jack felt a lump lodge in his throat. She was a romantic. Why hadn't he picked up on that? She was as romantic as he was.

Gloria and Ray were swamped with hugs, kisses and congratulations, beginning with heartfelt good wishes from Jack. Eddie turned the stereo on, and in a moment everyone was dancing—everyone but Caroline and Jack.

Caroline was thinking this was an appropriate moment to say her good-nights and make her escape, but in the next instant Jack was standing in front of her.

"Dance with me?" he asked quietly.

Before Caroline could quite decide how to answer, she was in his arms.

Jack led her slow dancing. Caroline's heart fluttered erratically, but thankfully he wasn't close enough to her for him to tell. He imagined they probably looked awkward as he made sure to keep his distance. But, hell, he was ill at ease.

"I did want to thank you..." Caroline began lamely, looking over his shoulder. "The kids had a very good time at the carnival. They were still talking about it this morning. They've never been on a Ferris wheel before. And, of course, the cotton candy..." She realized she was rambling on to hide her nervousness.

"I'm really glad they had a good time." He was forcing himself to breathe shallow, not to enjoy her familiar scent.

"Jack, couldn't we be friends?" *Please,* her voice asked.

"I don't know, Caroline." The idea depressed him. "All I do know is that if you've set out to confuse me, you've done a bang-up job."

"I don't know what you mean." She thought she was the only one who was feeling mixed up.

"I just love the earrings," Gloria said behind Caroline, where she and Ray swayed in place, talking to everyone who passed their way.

"I'm so glad." Caroline smiled, twisting her head toward the two. They looked like they were floating on air.

The warmth of Jack's hand spread against the small of Caroline's back. Her eyes drifted up to him. He'd watched through the evening how easily she'd made friends with his friends, and, though he had no right to it, it gave him a feeling of pride.

"Did you hear from Marty?" he asked, and knew instantly he'd said the wrong thing.

Caroline's back stiffened. "Not yet." She didn't bother to try for any optimism. "We really should discuss the house."

He didn't want to discuss the house. He couldn't have cared less about the house at the moment. "Not here," was all he said.

Caroline avoided his eyes. "I really should be going." She extricated herself from his hold, knowing without a doubt that ending it now was best for her. Their lawyers could settle their business dealings.

He wanted to stop her, but he didn't know what to say. Maybe it was just as well that they both cut their losses. For the life of him, he really couldn't figure her out.

Jack watched her say good-night to Gloria and Ray and then to all the others in the room. And it hurt him that she didn't make any effort to single him out.

He called it a night, himself, shortly after she left.

* * *

The phone started to ring as soon as she got into bed. Caroline picked the receiver up from her nightstand. "Hello."

Jack kneaded the back of his neck. "I really can act like a jackass sometimes. Caroline, I really would like us to be friends."

In the intense silence that followed, Caroline silently chided herself. *You asked him to be friends, now say something.*

"Good," she said. "Really."

"I want to talk to you, but not on the phone."

"Okay." She was holding her own with single-word responses. "Where?"

"Could you meet me for lunch tomorrow?"

"Yes."

"There's an Italian restaurant right down the street from my yard. Blue Moon. Is twelve all right?"

"Fine."

"I'll see you tomorrow."

"Yes. Well . . ." Caroline stammered. "Good night."

"Sleep well." For moments after she hung up, Jack held the receiver in his hand, unwilling to shake her voice from his mind. Friends? Just friends?

Jack, in jeans and a light blue shirt with the tail hanging out, was waiting outside the restaurant when Caroline arrived promptly at noon, looking arty in sandals, a billowy white cotton skirt and a long green polo. It had been cold out yesterday, but today it was warm again. Normal for the end of September.

"Hope you're hungry." He smiled.

"Famished," she fibbed.

Jack opened the door to the restaurant and held it for her. Blue Moon was small and crowded. The decor was typical—red-and-white checkered tablecloths and dark paneled walls, one decorated with a map of Italy overemphasized as a boot.

A hostess, middle-aged and harried, approached. "Smoking or nonsmoking?"

"Nonsmoking," Jack answered.

They were led to a table off to one side.

Caroline and Jack took seats. The hostess handed them each a menu. "The waiter will be by in a few minutes." She rushed off.

"They make the best spaghetti and meatballs," Jack suggested.

"That sounds good." Caroline spread her paper napkin on her lap.

"I want to talk to you about the house," Jack began, but was interrupted by a waiter who spotted their menus closed.

Caroline listened to Jack order their lunches. "Do you want cola with yours?" he asked.

Caroline nodded.

"I want to talk to you about the house, too," Caroline said after the waiter walked off.

"Let me go first," Jack insisted. "The deal I had going fell through." Actually, the deal hadn't fallen through. He just wasn't going to kill her dream. "And since money is not a problem for me, you don't even have to pay the rent. We can straighten all that out after you get a part." Jack leaned back in his seat, feeling good. He wasn't just going to be a friend . . . he was going to be her best friend.

Caroline's eyes sparked indignantly. "What are you doing?"

"I..." Jack's voice cracked, and he cleared his throat. "I'm trying to help you out." Why was she jumping on him for trying to do the right thing?

"I don't need your financial assistance. I don't accept financial assistance from anybody, not even my ex-husband. My grandmother left me some money. It's been enough to tide me over, and I still have enough to put down on a house. I wouldn't have tried to get back into acting if I didn't have something behind me."

"I'm sorry I misjudged your situation." Had he ever misjudged her, he realized, after having assumed that she'd taken her ex-husband for all she could get. "I was just trying to be a friend."

"Friend, my eye!" She hit him full force with a straight-on stare. "Exactly what do you expect from your most generous offer?"

Jack knew what she was getting at. Only he couldn't believe it... "I can assure you that I do not expect you to repay my offer over the house with any sexual favors."

"Are you this generous to all your friends?"

"Of course not." Jack was frustrated. "That's not the point."

"What is the point?"

She was carrying this thing too far. "The point is that I'm falling in love with you." Until that moment, Jack had no idea he was going to say those words.

"That is the biggest line in the books. Can't you come up with something more original?"

Jack was just about to respond to her latest sarcasm when the sky suddenly opened up for him. He was in love with her. He was crazy in love with her. It was as plain as the nose on his face. He'd just been too dumb to realize it before.

She didn't believe him. Not for one moment. "I'm not going to sit here and listen to any more of this." Angrily, Caroline pushed back her seat. She got to her feet and knocked into the waiter who had just approached with their lunches.

The waiter's tray teetered.

Aghast, Caroline watched, frozen.

Jack tried to duck to his side. But it didn't help. He got both their plates of spaghetti and meatballs in his lap.

Caroline threw her hands up. "I told you I was jinxed," she said lamely, and then walked out while the waiter ran for wet towels.

Jack drove straight over to the house after mopping himself up in the restaurant as best he could. His jeans weren't too bad, just damp in spots, but his shirt was splattered with spaghetti sauce. Wet towels hadn't done much to take out the stains.

Caroline answered the door to Jack's ring. "I want to talk to you," he said.

Caroline made no move to grant him entry. "Go ahead and talk."

"Do you want me to talk to you right here and possibly attract your neighbors?"

Caroline breathed a puff of air and then let him in the house. She did not want to be the talk of the neighborhood.

"Are the kids still in school?" Jack asked.

Caroline nodded.

"Myra?"

"Out shopping."

"Could we go and sit down?" They were still standing in the hallway.

Caroline led the way to the kitchen. Jack sat down at the table. Caroline remained on her feet. She struck a stiff pose with her back to the sink.

Jack smiled. "You really can be a little spitfire."

Caroline didn't think that required a response.

"For God's sake, Caroline... I am in love with you."

Caroline felt like she was on a railroad track and the train was coming. If she believed him and he wasn't telling the truth, meaning it with all of his heart, she might not be able to recover. "How can you be in love with me? We haven't even known each other that long."

"I guess there isn't a time frame for love. But I would have thought the way I was fighting it that it wouldn't have snuck up on me the way it did." He tried a smile on her, but she didn't respond to it. Instead, she ran out of the room.

Jack stood perplexed for a few seconds, and then he ran after her. He found her in the bathroom off her bedroom. She was holding a wad of toilet paper to her eyes.

"Caroline..." He said her name helplessly. The last thing he'd expected was for her to cry.

Caroline sniffled and wiped at her eyes. "Those stains are never going to come out of your shirt if you don't soak it."

Jack unbuttoned his shirt, took it off, dropped it on the sink and turned the water on. "Okay?"

Caroline sniffled again. "Marty called me this morning. I have a part."

"Oh, honey. That's great. Tell me about it." He took her lovely face in his broad hands while he dried her eyes with his thumbs.

Caroline smiled a quivering smile. "You're not going to believe this, but I'm going to play a woman who's divorced with two kids. And there's this guy in town who's a confirmed bachelor, but he falls in love with her."

"Does she fall in love with him?" Jack asked gently.

She didn't have any idea how the writers would develop her story line. "Yes, but she's terrified. She hasn't done very well in the romance department. Her first husband dumped her for someone younger."

Jack stroked and caressed her back. "Her first husband must have been a jerk."

"Well, he did have his hands full with her. Somehow or another, she always seemed to get herself into scrapes."

"I have a feeling this bachelor is going to love her scrapes." His hands locked around her waist, but he held her loosely, knowing she had more to say.

Caroline sniffed again. "This bachelor is also very career-minded. She wonders if he isn't like her first husband, who was more interested in making money than he was in her."

Unable to resist any longer, Jack kissed the corner of her mouth. "Her first husband was not only a jerk, he was also a fool."

"She acts silly sometimes." Caroline swayed closer to him. "But personally, I think there should be some silliness."

Jack kissed the tip of her nose. "Silly is my middle name."

"And romance... There should always be romance."

Jack teased her chin with his mouth. "Absolutely. There should always be romance."

Caroline started kissing Jack back, kiss for kiss. "I love you, Jack," she whispered.

"I know." Jack smiled.

Caroline's eyes flashed open. "What do you mean you know? This is my big scene...my moment."

Jack grinned. "I'm going to give you an even bigger moment. You see, this bachelor is going to ask her to marry him, and she says..." He handed her back the floor.

Caroline started crying too much to talk.

He held her hard against him, and she clung to him. He thought that if he lived to be a hundred he'd never tire of holding her close. "Oh, honey. Don't cry. And don't answer yet. Honestly, I can do this better."

Caroline looked up at him, wiping her cheeks with her knuckles. "Do you know what you're getting yourself into? Do you want a ready-made family? Do you want to put up with my jinxes?"

His feelings for her and the family he was going to inherit swelled inside him, bringing tears to his eyes. "I'm not a prize package, Caroline. But I'm going to be the best stepfather in the entire world. I love you, Caroline. I love your jinxes. I love every part of you. I love you because you're you." Jack smiled at her through his own tears. "This is a helluva room to propose in...."

Caroline smiled back at him. "It seems right for us."

Myra spotted Caroline and Jack entwined in the bathroom when she came upstairs and started to walk by Caroline's bedroom. But Myra didn't think that either of them needed to be rescued. Caroline looked like she had the situation well under control. And Jack wasn't doing too bad, either.... But did they realize that the water was running over the sink?

* * * * *